THE HOLE

ALSO BY HIROKO OYAMADA

The Factory

HIROKO
OYAMADA

THE HOLE

translated from the Japanese
by David Boyd

A NEW DIRECTIONS
PAPERBOOK ORIGINAL

The Hole was originally published in 2014 as *Ana* by Shinchosha Publishing Co., Tokyo. This English edition is published by arrangement with Shinchosha Publishing Co. in care of Tuttle-Mori Agency, Inc., Tokyo.

The translator would like to thank Rebekah Chacko for her generous assistance.

First published as New Directions Paperbook 1487 in 2020
Manufactured in the United States of America
Design by Erik Rieselbach

New Directions gratefully acknowledges the support of JAPANFOUNDATION.

Library of Congress Cataloging-in-Publication Data
Names: Oyamada, Hiroko, 1983– author. | Boyd, David, translator.
Title: The hole / Hiroko Oyamada ;
translated from the Japanese by David Boyd.
Other titles: Ana. English
Description: English language edition. |
New York : New Directions Publishing, 2020.
Identifiers: LCCN 2020021695 | ISBN 9780811228879 (paperback) |
ISBN 9780811228886 (ebook)
Classification: LCC PL874.Y36 A6513 2020 | DDC 895.63/6—dc23
LC record available at https://lccn.loc.gov/2020021695

8 10 9 7

New Directions Books are published for James Laughlin
by New Directions Publishing Corporation
80 Eighth Avenue, New York 10011

THE HOLE

I MOVED OUT HERE WITH MY HUSBAND. AT THE END OF May, we found out about the transfer. His new office was going to be in the same prefecture, but far from where he'd been working. A local branch office out in the country. It was the same area my husband was originally from, so he called his mother to see if she had any ideas about where we could live. "What about next door?" "Next door?" "The other house—the one we've been renting out. It just opened up." Her voice carried so well that I could hear every syllable from where I was sitting. The other house? Why hadn't I ever heard of this house before?

"A family of four had been living there, but they moved out in April. The Katos. They were so nice. When they left, they came by with a box of the most beautiful sumo mandarins. You met the Katos, right? They had a little boy with curly hair . . ." "No, I don't think so . . ."

On the memo pad on the table, I wrote SEPARATE HOUSE? I turned the pad toward my husband and he nodded. He grabbed the pen and wrote YES. TWO STORIES. His mother kept talking. "Anyway, they're gone now. We asked the realtor to find somebody new, but I guess they haven't gotten any bites. If you want it, I can call tomorrow and ask them to take the ad down. Sound good?" "How's the rent?" "Well, the Katos were paying 52,000 yen . . . But what do you think? Should I call the agent?"

My husband looked at me as if it was my decision. The timing couldn't have been better. We had to take it. I nodded. The rent was a lot less than our tiny apartment in the city—and we'd have an entire house to ourselves. "Sounds good. We can definitely afford 52,000." "What are you talking about? You won't need to pay anything." "Wait, what?" "Keep your money. Save it, for the future. I mean, we should probably think about taxes. We'll need to put something in writing, as a formality. Still, I don't want you paying us rent. We're family. The loan for that place is paid off now anyway. You know it's not the newest house, right?" My husband shot me the same look. I didn't have any issue with that. How could we be anything but grateful? Still, it was strange how I couldn't seem to picture this house—how big it was, what color it was, what the yard was like ... I must have seen it while visiting my husband's parents, but I was drawing a blank. I told myself that my inability to conjure any memory of the place probably meant it couldn't have been remarkably large or small. For whatever reason, I couldn't even recall what my husband's family home looked like. All I could remember were fragments—solar panels on the roof, a handful of trees out front. That was it.

"There's a parking space, right?" "One. You're going to need it, too. You know you'll need a car to live here, right? Otherwise you can't get around." "If I drive from there, I can probably make it to the office in under half an hour ... That should work. But, Mom, are you sure about the rent?" "Well, like I said, we'll have to sit down and do some paperwork, but really, don't worry about the money. Alright, it's settled. I'll call the agent first thing in the morning, okay?" "Sounds good, thanks. Asahi's going to need to quit her job, so anything we can save on rent will really help." "Asa's quitting?" his mother asked. Her voice was lower now, but just as audible. "Of course. That commute would never work." "Oh, I know, but what if she stayed there

About the Author and Contributors

Lesley Kamenshine, M.Ed., is a writer as well as a former journalist and columnist. She troubleshoots on behalf of groups with emerging concerns, seeking to understand their vision, then identifies and simplifies a path for success. She has written her second book, *Career Guide and Directory for Immigrant Professionals*, from the perspective of a career coach. While with the Montgomery Community College and U.S. Small Business Development Center in the 1990s, Ms. Kamenshine developed and implemented the award-winning Latino Business Support Program, the first of its kind in the Washington, D.C., region. Through a variety of activities, her goal has been and continues to be clarifying a path for immigrants pursuing their American Dream, although she has recently begun addressing the needs of the aging. Leslie Kamenshine continuously seeks to tackle uncommon ground.

Solveig Fisher has always been fascinated by language and has made it the focus of her career. With a B.A. in comparative language and an M.A. in linguistics from the University of Chicago, she began working in educational publishing, first as a pronunciation editor for the *Random House Dictionary* and subsequently as associate editor of languages and linguistics for *Encyclopaedia Britannica*. Both her study of languages and her editorial work prepared her well for teaching English as a second language. Through the years, she has taught ESL to many different populations in continuing education departments, college programs, corporations, and factories. She is currently an associate professor in the American English language program at Montgomery College–Germantown Campus. Solveig Fisher wrote the first chapter of this book.

Maureen Ickrath is a marketing manager at the Office of Workforce Development and Continuing Education at Prince George's Community College. She began pursuing her degree when her children were in college, thus understands firsthand the need to work while attending school. She used every nontraditional option available to speed up the education process and reduce costs. After receiving her B.S., she felt a compelling need to share what she had learned with other adult students. As a result, she developed a noncredit course entitled Poof! You're a College Graduate, to teach students about the myriad of nontraditional methods for gaining college credit, preventing frustration, staying motivated, and combining courses. Much of the course material is contained in the third chapter of this book. Maureen Ickrath also teaches a credit course to teach students how to document experiences outside the classroom, which can be evaluated for college credit. As a volunteer speaker, she shares her knowledge with women's groups, fraternal organization, clubs, religious groups, and other organizations.

Ruthe Kaplan, M.Ed. and Ed.S., has been a financial aid adminstrator at George Washington University and Montogmery College. She has worked with recent high school graduates, returning adult learners, and immigrants from all over the world striving to improve their lives through education. Ruthe Kaplan wrote the fourth chapter of this book.

Keke Lowe, B.A., is a native of Lesotho, an American citizen, and a fellow at the Economic Development Institute (EDI) of the World Bank. She spent six years working with international forums of the U.N. and the World Bank, and for the last ten years has provided career information to individuals and groups and maintained career center resources. She has also been involved with outreach efforts to ethnic and multicultural communities in Montgomery County. Keke Lowe is a diversity trainer for the National Multicultural Institute in Washington, D.C. She has contributed her expertise to the second chapter of this book.

and you moved out here on your own? I mean, this is her job we're talking about." My husband looked at me again; I shook my head. If he's moving, I'm moving. End of story. I'm not even a permanent employee. It's not the kind of job that's worth holding on to. My husband nodded at me, then said, "We'll make the move together." His mother laughed a little and said, "You two are still young, aren't you?" It wasn't like we were newlyweds or anything. Did she really believe my work was that important? I was almost jealous. She'd held on to the same job for most of her adult life and was only a year or two away from retirement. When she gave birth to her son, she only took six months off. And it's not like they needed the money. She could've spent more time at home, but that's how much she loved her job. I didn't feel the same way about mine. Although it wasn't the worst position out there, I'd hardly call it rewarding. I didn't hate it, but I wasn't exactly thrilled to be there, either. To be honest, the job was a little too demanding, considering how little I was paid. Sure, it was the sort of work anyone could do, but I wasn't so young or naïve to let that bother me.

My husband placed the receiver in the cradle and smiled. "You heard that, right? What do you think? Too close?" "To what? Your family?" "Well, your mother-in-law." When he said the word, I almost laughed out loud. I guess I hadn't thought of her that way. She was better than that. Of course, she wasn't perfect, but her virtues easily outnumbered her faults. She was warm, caring, and hardworking. I'd probably feel differently about her if we had to live under the same roof, but I could handle being neighbors. "I don't mind. It sounds like a good situation for us. Besides, who knows how long it'll take me to find a job up there? If we can get by without paying rent ..." "Yeah, you're right about that." My husband grinned, pulled his cell phone out of his pocket, and ran his fingers across the screen. "But what about you?" I asked. "Are you okay being that close to home?" We weren't very far away from his parents as things were, but he'd never seemed too excited about going home for the holidays. My own parents were a bit farther away, which made it relatively easy to get out of family gatherings. Some years, I had to come up with excuses, telling them we were traveling or something like that. "Not at all. At this age, it actually feels right." "Feels right?" My husband smiled at something on his phone, then glanced up at me. Unlike me, my husband had a lot of friends. I watched his fingers glide over the surface of his phone. He was probably telling some friend about the move. *I'm moving into the house next to my parents . . . No rent!* "I don't know. My parents aren't that young anymore. Who knows how long Grandpa's going to be around? It'll be good to be closer to them." "Yeah . . ." I unmuted the TV and laughter filled the room. I brought the volume down as quickly as I could. On the screen, a group of half-naked people with brown skin were running in a field, chasing after a large animal. I had no idea where they were, but it wasn't Japan. They had white and yellow markings on their faces and chests. It could've been paint—or maybe tattoos. Apparently, the animal belonged to them. It was dragging around some kind of rope tied to its leg. Among the people—all of them in shorts—stood a chubby, pasty-faced Japanese comedian in a grass skirt. "And of course you're coming with me. Of course you are." "Does your mom think I'm a permanent employee or something?" "No, she knows you're not." His fingers were sliding over his phone with even greater speed. He was probably writing an email. There was a time when I would have wanted to know what he was up to, but not anymore. As long as he wasn't doing anything sexual or criminal, there was no need for me to get involved.

"By the way, did you tell them you're quitting?" "Work? Yeah, today." "What'd they say?" "Nothing," I said with a wry smile. He tilted his head to the side, eyes still fixed on his phone.

"After everything you've done for them?" "Well, yeah. It's not like I was doing anything that important. After we move, I hope I can find something better. It's probably going to be part-time, right? I wish I could find a permanent position ... Then again, I'm turning thirty this year, so ..." "But we won't have to worry about rent up there, so what's the rush?" "Yeah, I guess you're right." Just then, on the TV, the comedian lunged at the wayward animal but fell short, landing face-first in a puddle of mud. Glancing up at the screen, my husband muttered "idiot" and laughed. I laughed, too. We moved into our new home two weeks later.

"QUITTING? ARE YOU SERIOUS?" I WAS IN THE BATHROOM with my only friend from work. A sheet of blotting paper pressed against her forehead, she widened her eyes in disbelief when I broke the news. "My husband's getting transferred to another branch. We're moving . . ." "You serious? Where to?" "Not far. North of here, but too far to commute . . . I know, right? It's kind of sudden . . ." "No, I'm happy for you . . . Is it okay to say that?" She tossed the used sheet in the trash and let out an exaggerated sigh. It was the busiest part of the year, but a good portion of the permanent staff was nowhere to be seen. One had just had a child, another was sick, and two others simply couldn't face coming in. The extra work had to be done—by us, the non-permanent employees. We were both putting in overtime, even though it wasn't in our contracts. We were even handling tasks outside of our job descriptions—receiving orders, interacting with clients—but our base pay remained the same. The only appreciation our employers ever showed us came when the permanent employees got their winter bonuses. Instead of bonuses, we got envelopes with A SMALL TOKEN OF OUR GRATITUDE printed on the front in a cursive script. It really wasn't much. From what I'd heard, the permanent employee bonus was three months' pay—at a minimum—but I only got 30,000 yen, in cash. I did the math. Permanent employees likely got somewhere between 600,000 and 700,000. My envelope had maybe a twentieth of that. It's always nice to feel appreciated, right? I dropped the envelope into my bag, where it's been ever since. I never felt the urge to spend or even deposit it. Who knows—if I were sticking around, maybe I'd get 50,000 next year. Maybe.

"I wish I could leave ... I wish I could quit," she said. She was two or three years older than me and lived with a guy she wanted to marry. He had a permanent position somewhere, but still wasn't making much money. She didn't like her job, but didn't know what else she could do. It was horrible being worked to the bone, but there was no guarantee that she'd find anything better elsewhere. "Really, what are the chances I'd find something permanent out there? At least I'm full-time here. And if we keep working overtime like this, I'll end up making more than my boyfriend. Not that there's any hope of ever getting promoted to a permanent position here ..." When she first started working, she was a permanent employee at a major corporation, but her boss was an evil scumbag who made her life hell. She resigned and came here. "I'd give my right arm to never come back to this place. I wish someone would ask my boyfriend to transfer ... But what are you going to do? Look for something new up there?" "Well, it's way out in the country. I'll try to find something, but who knows. Either way, we should be all right. We're going to live in a house that my husband's family owns." "Wait, seriously? You mean you're going to be a housewife?" Her eyes opened even wider. "Look at you!" "Look at what?" "You, Matsuura-san. Living the dream. You won't have to work. You'll be free to look after the house, bake, do a little gardening ... That's the life." She shook her head as she tugged at the bottom of her vest, smoothing it with both hands. Then she held her nails up to her face, inspecting them closely. Once a month, she went to the salon to have them done—and it looked like she was almost due for her next trip. These were the kind of nails you had to go to the salon to remove. It probably wasn't conscious, but she had a habit of picking at them. They were dark purple and studded with tiny, clear rhinestones, but at this point only one-third of her nails had any color left. It looked a little punk rock. She told me it was 6,000 yen for both hands (rhinestones cost extra), but she knew somebody at the salon, so she didn't have to pay full price. I'd done my own nails before, but didn't take good care of my cuticles, so they never looked very good. Still, I never felt the need to spend that kind of cash to have somebody glue little stones to my fingernails.

"What I wouldn't give to be a housewife ... Wait, no way. Are you pregnant?" I shook my head. She was basically the only person I ever spoke to at the office. I had no idea how to interact with the permanent staff, and it didn't help that I was shy. Even though she was my closest work friend, that didn't mean that we were actually close. She was always telling me about the things that were worrying her—how she and her boyfriend kept putting off marriage and how she was scared that she was going to miss her window to have a baby. I wasn't pregnant—not that I would tell her if I were. She washed her hands, then wiped her fingers with extra care, as if polishing the stones. The color on her nails never seemed to last, but those little gemstones stayed put no matter what. "Okay, not yet. But once you move and you have some time on your hands, I bet you'll get pregnant in no time. You have to tell me, okay? Seriously, I don't care how far away you live. I'll come visit."

I don't know why, but she'd always been under the impression that I wanted a child as badly as she did. I'm pretty sure she thought I'd been trying to get pregnant ever since I got married but wasn't having any luck. I suppose I could've said something to set the record straight, but I just went along with it. The truth was I wasn't trying to have children—not that I was bitterly opposed to the idea. I always figured, if it happens, it happens. "If you're going to have a baby, you're better off working. That way you get support from the government." "Support?" "Well, you wouldn't get all the benefits you'd receive if you were permanent, but still . . ." She leaned in to get a better look at her eyebrows in the mirror. For someone who spent as much money as she did on her nails, I thought it was strange how little makeup she wore. Then again, she had such strong features that it was probably best not to overdo it. She had wide double eyelids, long eyelashes that cast shadows over her cheeks, a giant mole by her temple, and skin far better than most, but she had so many fillings that you couldn't help but notice all the metal when she smiled. "It's definitely best if you're both permanent. I mean, socially and personally." "So if you had another shot at a permanent position, you'd take it?" "Me? In a heartbeat!" She nodded aggressively. During lunch, all the permanent women go outside to eat. Meanwhile, the rest of us eat at our desks. It's an unspoken rule. Permanents would only eat at their desks when they were exceptionally busy or if something was going on with their usual lunch partner. It's not like the permanents and non-permanents despised each other. Some permanents were actually nice. We simply lived in different worlds. They were taking home 600,000-yen bonuses, while our envelopes contained only a fraction of that. What could we possibly talk about? The bathroom was quiet. Just the two of us. In another fifteen minutes, the permanent employees would flock to the sinks to brush their teeth before getting started on the afternoon work.

"I mean, it's not fair," she said, her voice echoing. "We're doing the same work as them, right? So what's the deal with these stupid envelopes? I want a bonus, a real bonus. Yeah, I'd take a permanent position. And I'd go to all the lunch meetings, do all the business trips. At least I'd get maternity leave. What do I have now? Think about it: What if I got pregnant and they let me go right before I had the baby? Then what if there was an opening a year or so later and they took me back? They'd hire me as a part-timer, right? That'd be the best I could hope for. And if there was no opening, I'd get nothing, obviously. But what if I was permanent? I could take a year off, work limited hours for the next three after that, collect every bonus and paycheck—even if it's not the full amount—and even get financial support from the government. Come on! Are we even human? I'd definitely do it. You really wouldn't take a permanent spot if they offered you one?" "I don't know. I guess I don't like the idea of being any busier than I already am . . ." "By the way, what did you get for overtime last month?" She turned her head toward me. I could smell her minty toothpaste—mintier than mine. "About what I was expecting." "I got maybe 70,000." "Same here." We were only paid for what we reported in thirty-minute blocks. Whatever didn't fit in those blocks was lost. I reported everything I could last time, and the amount was larger than what I was used to seeing, but it didn't bring me any joy. The figure under "base pay" was exactly what it had been. "It's crazy if you think about what we usually make. Compared to a month without overtime, we're making almost fifty percent more, right? But they're having us do a lot more work, right? Let's face it. We're corporate slaves. I mean, we're not even permanent." "But the overtime definitely helps." "Oh, I know. My boyfriend doesn't get paid for overtime. The grass is never greener, right? But I don't have time to make us dinner anymore. I think my boyfriend's about to snap. Nothing but premade dinners from the supermarket every night . . . Hey, what have you been eating?" "Curry—four nights in a row. I guess I've been making a lot of soups and stews. That's it, though . . ." "Ha, you deserve an award. I mean, you're still cooking. Can I tell you something? Sometimes, just sometimes, when my boyfriend gets home before me, I wish that he'd have dinner waiting for me. Does your husband ever make you dinner?" "Not really. I mean, he would, if I asked . . . But, how can I put it . . ." While I searched for the words, she faced the mirror, glared at herself, and said, "Oh, I get it. Believe me. I never say anything either. I think it—but I never say it. Like, 'Come on. It's your turn.' Sometimes I wonder what's stopping me. Maybe I'd feel better about it if I had a permanent position. Maybe not. I don't know . . ."

I looked down at my watch. It's important to get some rest during lunch to keep from dropping dead, but I was ready to get back to work. I was going to have to stay late again today—and probably every day until I left. "So, wait, when you leave, who's going to do your share of the work?" I looked at her in the mirror. She was holding her hand out, scrutinizing the stones on her nails. "I need to go back to the salon. I think I'll use my overtime pay to get a few more rhinestones," she muttered. White spots of water had dried on the mirror, covering her body from the chest down.

WE MOVED IN ON A SUNDAY—AND THE ONLY DAY IT rained in an otherwise dry rainy season. In some areas, the river flooded and people had to evacuate their homes. When the movers came early that morning, they looked as though they felt sorry for us, but we felt sorrier for them. They were the ones who had to carry our furniture in the heavy rain. Once all of our belongings had been loaded onto the truck, my husband and I got into our car. He put on some music, something between jazz and new age. I was asleep before I knew it. When I woke up, we were already there, parked in front of my husband's family home. His mother, Tomiko, was standing by the door. It seemed like the rain was coming down even harder than when we'd left. It was so dark out that it could have been the middle of the night.

As they got out of the truck, the movers nodded to Tomiko while giving questioning looks to me and my husband. Before we could say a word, Tomiko asked, "You're going to sleep upstairs, right?" She was wearing jeans and a T-shirt with the sleeves rolled up, her round, babyish forearms showing. "Uh . . ." "Asa, did you just wake up?" As I rubbed the corner of my eye, a stray eyelash got caught under my fingernail. "Yeah, Muneaki did the driving . . . Sorry." "Oh, it's fine. I'm sure it was just the packing. That kind of work takes more out of us women. So—sleeping upstairs?" "Yeah, that's what I was thinking. Why?" "I told you over the phone about the curtains, right? The Katos left theirs up. I took them down and washed them this morning, but I had no idea it was going to be raining all day. We can't dry them like this. How about staying at our house tonight? Or I could run over to the laundromat and use the dryers there. It's not too far from here. Just a quick drive." "We'll be fine without curtains." The mover leaned in and quietly asked, "Who's she?" "Oh, that's my husband's mother. She lives next door." "Oh, okay," he said, smirking. The smell of his sweat mixed with the rain. The hair showing from under his hat was wet, but his uniform was completely dry. Maybe it was sweatproof.

The movers started unloading and Tomiko took command immediately. "Are you boys doing this part-time? This weather is the worst, isn't it? I put mats down in the entryway, so come on in . . ." In the house, the movers took off their shoes, revealing bright white socks, then stepped inside carrying wall and floor guards under both arms. My husband's mother showed them around the house. "Over here's the closet. That's the kitchen. West is this way, so this room gets a lot of sunlight. Oh, maybe you don't need these, but I brought them over to put under the furniture, to hold everything in place. You know, for earthquakes. What do you think? Do you need them?" The movers looked at my husband, who glanced at me. "Thank you, that's great. We didn't bring any." As always, my husband's mother was extremely well prepared. She had brought over a cooler stocked with plastic bottles of tea and vitamin water. She also had a few big bags with towels, duct tape, a tape measure, and some other useful items. She reached into one of the bags and pulled out a blue package with SIR GRIPS-A-LOT printed on the front. She handed it to the movers and asked, "You know how to use these, right? With anything heavy—the fridge, things like that—just slip these under it, nice and tight." "Great, thanks." "How many do you need? I brought seven. Did you bring any bookshelves?"

"No ..." "Okay. So, you have your fridge, cabinet ... Did you bring a dresser?" "A dresser..? Uh, yes." "Okay. Are you going to keep it upstairs?" My husband's phone rang. "Sorry, I need to take this." He stomped upstairs, his phone already up to his ear. His mother watched him go, then looked at me and shrugged. I bet most people would think she's still in her forties. She never wore much makeup, but her cheeks were a healthy red. My mother was probably ten years younger than Tomiko, but definitely looked older. On some level, I guess I thought this was because my own mother became a full-time housewife when she had me. Tomiko was still working. I could hear my husband laughing. Tomiko dabbed at the sweat forming on her forehead. "He should be in charge of this. Well, I guess we'll have to sort things out without him. Okay—how about putting the dresser upstairs?"

The movers spread protective mats over the stairs and down the hallways. Tomiko brought out a pair of slippers. "Asa, why don't you put these on? I did some cleaning before you got here, but still ... By the way, I had professional cleaners come in, too. You're all set now. Mildewproof and miteproof." Maybe that was why it smelled like chlorine. "We appreciate it." "The Katos did a great job of keeping the place clean, so it was easy ... They had a little boy, but his mother kept a real close eye on him. You know how kids are always putting stickers on everything? Well, I was worried we'd end up with cartoon stickers on every surface, but look around. Spick-and-span, right?" "Where's Grandpa today?" "Pretty sure he's sleeping. He was watching TV a little while ago. He's in front of the TV all day, nodding off ..." "What about Dad? Is he home?" "No, he's on another overnight golf trip. You didn't see the Atenza out front, did you? Talk about bad timing, with this rain and all ..." My husband's parents had two cars: a dark-blue compact and a larger silver midsize. I guess the bigger one belonged to my father-in-law. I'd never spent much time with him. He came to our engagement party and wedding. I'd see him when we visited over the holidays, but Tomiko did most of the talking. He'd never left much of an impression on me. He was past retirement age, but was still working in some capacity, although the details were never clear to me. One of the movers sprinted toward us. "Sorry, excuse me, Matsuura-san ..." "Yes?" my husband's mother answered before I could respond. "Where do you want the microwave? Should we plug it in next to the fridge? What about the rice cooker?" "Well, let's take a look." Before I could say anything, my husband's mother had run into the kitchen with the movers. My husband was laughing even harder upstairs. "I'm telling you, it's really coming down. But that's my luck for you. I mean, how many times in your life do you make a big move like this? Of course, I had to move on the one day we get flood warnings. Hey, welcome to my life, right? Heh." I was alone, standing by the open front door. The rain didn't reach me, but I could feel the moist air. The smell of chlorine mixed with the acidic smell from outside. I looked at the doorstop the movers had put down, then looked at my feet. The slippers had a dog face stitched over the toes with a pink tongue sticking out. They were really comfy. They had to be brand new. Did she buy them for me? Was she going to take them back after the move? "Hey, Asa, can you come here a second?" As I walked toward the kitchen, the dog's ears flopped with every step. I hurried through the living room, over the smooth floor, and into a kitchen that was much bigger than the one I was used to. Looking out the big window, I saw a garden that couldn't have been more than ten feet wide. I didn't see any plants, only some puddles and a few holes that appeared to be man-made. Maybe the Katos took their plants with them when they left—or maybe the boy ripped everything up before they moved out. Through the rain, I could see the outline of Tomiko's garden next door. For a second, I thought I saw a person standing in the trees, but when I tried to get a better look, nothing was there. "Is there something . . ." "No, it's fine. We just figured it out. So we'll have the fridge over here and the kitchen cabinet will go over here, okay?" The movers gave me blank looks, waiting for an answer. I put on a big smile and said, "Sounds good!"

The rain was still coming down as we went to sleep that night. When I woke up in the morning, I went over to the upstairs window and took down the brand-new bath towels that Tomiko had used to cover the windows the night before. I could see the dry, white sky. I had woken up earlier than usual, but it was already bright out. For a second, I felt as though we'd moved someplace far away, a place where the days and seasons follow an entirely different rhythm. The Scandinavian midnight sun came to mind, but we hadn't left Japan. We hadn't even left the prefecture. We were only slightly closer to the mountains. I guess we'd moved to a new town—but this place was barely big enough to call a town. What was the postcode here? It really was bright outside. Judging from the sun, it looked like it could have been noon, but when I checked the clock, it wasn't even six yet. I looked back at my husband. Still asleep. I cracked the window open, and the buzz of brown cicadas filled the room. Cicadas. The first I'd heard this year. And with that, the rainy season was brought to an unceremonious end. Summer had arrived.

THERE WAS A RIVER A SHORT WALK FROM THE HOUSE. IT was miles from the ocean, but still fairly wide and muddy in places. I don't know why, but I thought if we were this close to the river we would have cooler summers. I was wrong. Even when the river was out of sight, the pungent smell of grass and stagnant water was overwhelming. On the other side of the river was a mountain, half of which was covered with gray houses. It looked like a new development. I bet some of the homes were still for sale. I'd seen their banners around town: MISONO GARDENS: YOUR NEW LIFE IS WAITING FOR YOU. My husband took the car to work every morning, so the only way for me to get around was to walk or take the bus. Except during rush hour, the bus came only once every sixty minutes, and it was a forty-minute ride to the train. And I wasn't desperate to meet up with old friends or go shopping, so I ended up staying home most of the time.

If I did go out, I'd usually just walk to the supermarket and back. It was the peak of summer, and I tried to avoid walking around in the middle of the day. The supermarket opened early in the morning—maybe because it was summer, or maybe because most of the people in the area were old. After seeing my husband off and eating breakfast, I'd go shopping for groceries. It was clear from the size of the parking lot that they were expecting most shoppers to drive. But early in the morning the store was deserted. At around nine or ten, it got really crowded. Even the parking lot was a zoo. The middle-aged couples evidently hated pushing their shopping carts, weighed down with giant bags, all the way to their cars, so usually the husband would pull the car around front. It was far worse on weekends, when they had their weekly sales. The lot would fill up, with cars spilling out into the street. Shopping first thing in the morning sometimes meant going without certain items like meat or fish, but that was a small price to pay for avoiding big crowds and the walk home under the intense heat of the summer sun. Once I was finished at the supermarket, I'd spend the rest of the day at home. There were no libraries or malls or bookstores within walking distance. Once we'd finished moving in, I felt like a kid on summer vacation: no homework, no plans. I started looking for a job, but I was having trouble getting around. All I could do was check the bulletin boards at the grocery store and the other small businesses in the area. Under these circumstances, I couldn't imagine finding anything very soon. I'd wake up a little before six, pack my husband's lunch, make his breakfast, see him off, go shopping, clean the house, or maybe run the laundry—but, after that, I didn't have anything to do. Living the dream? Really? It was weird to think about how, until now, I'd been working from morning till night. That life didn't seem real anymore. We were two different people: the me who had to work all day to make ends meet, and the me who had nothing to do after lunch except waste time until making dinner in the evening. I was pretty sure I'd get sick of my new routine within a week—but it only took a day. Every day after that was as mind-numbing as the one before, ad infinitum. In theory, I could watch TV, use the computer, read a book, bake like I used to when I was single—but it seemed like everything cost money. I had to spend money to pass the time. People say housewives get free room and board and even time to nap, but the truth is napping was the most economical way to make it through the day. The hours moved slowly, but the days passed with staggering speed. Soon I lost all sense of time. I didn't have any appointments or deadlines. The days were slipping through my fingers.

When I opened the windows, I could hear the cicadas. Maybe it was the weather, or maybe it was all the trees in the area, but I'd never heard so many cicadas in my life. Their cries were so close that I wondered if they were coming from inside me—if maybe I'd swallowed one. After only a second, I would get used to the noise, but when something changed and I could feel their cries on my skin again, it made me feel like I was going to suffocate. It wasn't very loud when the windows were shut, but I needed to keep the windows open to get some fresh air. I wasn't bringing in any money, so it didn't feel right to blast the AC when I was the only one at home. How could I allow myself to nap in air-conditioned bliss when my husband was sweating at his desk?

I was half-asleep on the couch when I got a call from an unknown number. I sat up, stared at the numbers for a second or two, then pressed ACCEPT. "Hey, Asa, do you have a minute?" It was Tomiko, but her voice was different from the way it sounded at home. It was lower, drier. "I'm really, really sorry about this. There's something I had to take care of this morning, but I didn't get around to it. Well, it's not that I didn't get around to it. I guess I forgot." "Forgot about what?" "There's some money I need to deposit today, but I left it in an envelope at home. It's ready to go. The deposit slip is in there, too, filled out and everything. The problem is, if I do it when I get home, it'll be too late. It has to be in by five, six at the latest. I really need it to be in on time, so I was thinking about leaving work early ... But I thought I'd ask you first. Could I ask you to take care of it? Are you busy today?" She sounded weirdly polite. Maybe she had coworkers nearby. But was there anyone else around? It was abnormally quiet on the other end of the line—nothing but the sound of her voice. I bet her work was nice and air-conditioned. I'd been on the verge of falling asleep, but I had to get up and open the curtains to get a breeze going, then close them again because it was too bright outside. A headache was starting to spread around my temples, humming with the cicadas. I heard something that sounded like a child screaming. It was early July—too early for summer vacation—so the child had to be too young for school. It was an oddly full scream for a child that age. I tried to focus on the phone. "I'll take care of it," I said. The day before, I'd taken the bus to the train, then went all the way to the dentist to deal with a cavity, but that was over now. I didn't have any plans today. Not today—or any other day for the foreseeable future. Morning, noon, and night, weekdays and weekends, I had nothing but time. Tomiko took a deep breath, then exhaled slowly. "What a relief. Thanks. So—the envelope's somewhere in the house. I'm not sure where I left it, but there aren't too many places it could be. It's either on the shelf by the door, on the kitchen table, or on the low table in the altar room. Like I said, the slip's in there with the money. Do you think you could take it down to the convenience store?" "The convenience store?" "That'd be easiest. It's a whole lot closer than the bank. You know where it is, don't you? The tiny 7-Eleven by the river . . ." "I know where it is." "Okay. You sure? Sorry to ask you to do this. I guess I had a lot of things on my mind this morning and didn't realize I'd forgotten it back at the house. I can't really ask Grandpa to take care of this, you know? It involves money and it's hot out. You have no idea how much this helps. It's really hot out there, Asa. Be careful, okay? Why don't you take the change and buy yourself some ice cream for the trip back? Actually, you'd better finish the ice cream first, then walk home, okay? Otherwise, it'll melt." By the end of the call, it almost seemed like she thought she was giving directions to a small child.

When we got off the phone, I looked at my screen. "SAVE NUMBER?" It had to be Tomiko's work number. Of course I didn't have it. I didn't even have her cell number. How did she get mine? Did she ask my husband? Why didn't she just call the home phone? She knew I'd be here. After thinking about it for a few seconds, I decided I'd better keep her number. It couldn't hurt to have a way to reach her. I typed in TOMIKO (WORK), then pressed SAVE. As I typed, it occurred to me that I had no idea where she worked. I didn't even know what kind of job she had.

I put my phone away and headed next door. The heat was brutal. Everything was perfectly still, no wind at all. Grandpa was out front, watering the plants. He was wearing a big straw hat and gripping a glistening green hose. He noticed me by the gate and raised a friendly hand in my direction. Grandpa's the only person at home during the day. He had to be close to ninety—maybe older—but he seemed to be in good health. "How are you doing today, Grandpa?" He didn't answer, but raised his hand higher in the air. He was smiling, showing his teeth. At the corners of his mouth, his metallic canines glinted in the sun. "It's hot out, isn't it?" What's he doing outside anyway? Tomiko said he spent his days in the house, napping in front of the TV—but what if that was only on weekends, when she was around? What if he spent the weekdays gardening when no one was home? They had a pine tree by the gate, a crape myrtle closer to the house, and a few other trees I couldn't name. The garden was full of all sorts of plants—some flowering, others that looked dead. Something deep green was growing in a planter, probably basil. It didn't look like anything you'd want to eat, like it might stain your teeth green if you bit into it. "Tomiko asked me to grab something for her. I'm going in, okay?" He kept smiling with all his teeth, but didn't say a word. He was definitely healthy for his age, but his ears weren't what they used to be. I smiled back at him as I rattled the door open and stepped inside.

Uncluttered by shoes, the entryway looked wider than usual. Coming in from the sun, the hallway was dark, even with the lights on. Once my eyes adjusted, I could see there was no envelope on the shelf. I stepped out of my shoes and headed for the kitchen. No envelope on the table, either. Everything was in its place: there was only a chopstick rest, thick-sliced bread with cheese, a couple of things wrapped in plastic, an apple sliced in quarters inside a Tupperware, and a thermos. That had to be Grandpa's lunch. On the wall by the sink were all kinds of implements arranged by height, and on the stove were a couple of pots and a frying pan that had been washed and dried. Down to one final option, I slid open the door to the altar room. Sunlight was shining through the shoji. Inside, a brown paper rectangle was waiting on the low table. I looked inside. Everything was there—the money and the slip. Once I was in the room, it didn't feel right to leave without paying my respects. As I put my hands together and faced the altar, I caught the smell of peaches. As I took a better look, I noticed the altar door was open, and there were three well-ripened peaches inside.

Photos of family members who had passed away lined the lintel. Only one was in color: Grandma's. The rest were black-and-white images of people who had made it to old age. When I came here to meet the family before getting married—or maybe right after—I looked up at that color photo and said to Tomiko, "I can really see the resemblance." "Between..?" Unsure of what to call the woman in front of me, I gestured at her with my right hand. "Between her and me?" When I nodded, Tomiko opened her eyes wide, then laughed with her whole body. "Asa, you're joking, right? I can't tell. You know that's my husband's mother . . ." "Oh,

I," I stuttered, then covered my mouth. "I don't know what I was thinking . . . I'm sorry." But the more I studied that photograph, the clearer it was—the two women definitely resembled each other. The lines around their mouths were identical. Maybe it wasn't about any specific feature. I just couldn't shake the feeling that they were related by blood. Tomiko finally stopped laughing, wiped the tears from her eyes, then sighed. "You're a funny one, aren't you?" "Really, I'm sorry . . ." "Why? I'm honored. Grandma was a beautiful woman in her day. Even when she was in her casket, her skin glowed like she was alive. You know she was named 'Miss Prefecture,' right? That was before the war . . ." Tomiko started laughing again. I took another look at the oddly angled photo—Grandma was looking down at me in her black kimono. The image was grainy, as if they'd taken a much smaller photo and had it enlarged. Still, the resemblance between them was undeniable. I nodded at the photo, then walked out of the room, envelope in hand.

When I left the house, Grandpa looked up and posed the same as before, hand raised high in the air. "Tomiko asked me to run this down to the store. I'll be back later." Still no answer. I had no idea what volume to use when talking to him. Whenever Tomiko spoke to him, he nodded—or even gave full responses—so he couldn't be completely deaf. I never had the impression that she was speaking any louder with him than anyone else. Maybe there was some secret to it—an ideal tone or speed. He stared at me for a couple of seconds, then turned away and started watering again.

I went back to our house to grab a few things and shut the windows. I slipped my wallet and Tomiko's envelope into my bag, put on my hat, and left. As I started to walk, it seemed like nothing around me was moving. The trees were as still as in a photograph, and the windows of all the houses were shut tight. There were no people around. No cats, no dogs, no crows. There wasn't a single sparrow in the sky. My eyes were tingling from the heat. Once the water from Grandpa's hose was too far away to hear, the only sound left was the cicadas: brown cicadas and another kind I don't think I'd ever heard before. The heat from the asphalt passed through the soles of my shoes, filling the space between my toes.

I KNEW WHERE THE 7-ELEVEN WAS, BUT HADN'T BEEN there since the move. Everything I needed was at the supermarket, and that was closer. I never bought magazines or made copies. The walk between our house and the 7-Eleven was probably beautiful in the right season. There were even a couple of signs describing the view when migratory birds visited in the winter, but it was summer, and no matter how scenic it was, a paved path in the middle of this heat was too much to take. The lack of breeze wasn't helping, either. The cries of the cicadas made the air feel even stickier. To the right of the path was the river, and to the left was a row of houses, each with its own garden and walls covered in goya and other vegetables. Beyond the leaves and vines, no signs of life. No one was making a sound—no TVs, no vacuums, no children. The riverbank was covered with grass, and so were parts of the river. There were a few birds on the water. They looked like herons, large and gray. The place was overgrown with susuki, kudzu, and other kinds of grass I'd seen before but couldn't name. Parts of the river were murky blue, stagnant green, or totally black from the blinding sunlight. The dry grass almost smelled baked. There was a big pile, brown and wet, on the path in front of me, probably left by a dog. On top of it were a couple of silver flies. For them, it was a mountain of food. It got me wondering—what would it feel like to sink your limbs and face into your lunch like that? Even the flies weren't moving. Maybe they were dead, knee-deep in dog crap. I kept an eye on the path as I walked. I passed a half-eaten Cup Noodles, an empty box of tissues, a work glove, a broken mosquito coil, and a few other sun-bleached artifacts. The cicada cries drilled into me with every breath I took. How many were there? How far can the cry of a cicada reach? I didn't see any dead cicadas around, but spotted a few abandoned husks along the path. From the sound of it, the area had to be full of them. It's not like they lived very long, so where were all the bodies? Just then, a grasshopper as big as my fist leapt from the bushes onto the path. It quivered as it folded its wings. It crept closer, then spread its wings and jumped away. When I looked up at the path ahead, I saw a big black animal.

At first, I thought the extreme heat was making me hallucinate, but the creature was really there. It was obviously a mammal—but not one I'd ever seen before. What I saw wasn't a weasel, and it wasn't a raccoon. It had to be as large as a retriever, maybe bigger. It had wide shoulders, slender and muscular thighs, but from the knees down, its legs were as thin as sticks. The animal was covered in black fur and had a long tail and rounded ears. Its ribs were showing, but its back was bulky, maybe with muscle or with fat. Slowly, it moved down the path ahead of me, barely casting a shadow, probably because the sun was right overhead. There were no birds, no dogs, no cats—just this black animal. I could see cars on the street on the other side of the river, but it was too bright to see the faces of the drivers or passengers inside. I was sure they couldn't see me or the animal. It wasn't looking at me, either. It was walking ahead of me, almost guiding me. And it didn't seem to mind being followed—it didn't look back and didn't speed up. I couldn't hear anything except the droning cicadas. I couldn't hear the river or the cars. After some time, the animal turned toward the river, cutting through the tall grass in a spot that had been well trampled. Without thinking, I did the same. As it headed down the slope, I heard something like clopping. Maybe it had hooves. The black water ahead of me glimmered in the sun. The grass clung to my skin as I walked, crushing things as I went. Plants, trash, crap, flies. They all broke or bent underfoot. Over the cicadas, I could hear a child shouting gleefully in the distance. There were old magazines and empty cans strewn among the weeds, but by this point they seemed to be as much a part of the riverbank as everything else. I saw the animal's tail slip through the grass, and I leapt after it, but there was nothing there to catch me.

I fell into a hole. It was probably four or five feet deep, but I'd managed to land on my feet. I looked around the grass—now at eye level—but the animal was nowhere to be found. I heard the grass rustling nearby, but before long the sound stopped.

At the edge of the hole, a click beetle flew up toward my face. When it landed, I could see streaks running down its black shell. The antennae on its head looked bent. It was making a clicking noise, but I couldn't tell where the sound was coming from. As I tried to move, I realized how narrow the hole really was. The hole felt as though it was exactly my size—a trap made just for me. The bottom of the hole was covered with something dry, maybe dead grass or straw. Looking toward the river through a break in the grass, all I could see was white light. The beetle flew away. I couldn't hear it anymore. The cicadas were the only sound. Cicadas cry to find a mate. They hear other cicadas crying around them and use what they hear to choose a partner. To my human ear, they sounded like a bunch of machines, a spray of emotionless noise. Maybe that's how we sound to them, too. I wasn't hurt. I wasn't even uncomfortable. I could smell something, maybe the grass or the river. I let it fill my lungs and body. There were a few rocks and bits of plastic on the flat grass surrounding the hole. I could see some black ants and red ants in lines, soldiering around. Their lines broke apart and intersected, the tiny red ones marching over the bodies of the larger black ones. My bag was there, near the ants. Most of them went around it, but a few crawled over it. I grabbed the bag and shook the ants loose, then checked inside to make sure everything was still there. Nothing was missing. A black ant took one of the red ones in its mandibles while other red ones bit its legs. The red ones looked softer than the black ones. I could feel the top of my head starting to bake in the sun. I had to get out of this hole, but it didn't look like it was going to be easy. I put my hands palm-down at the edge of the hole, and tried pushing myself up, but I barely got off the ground. My heart sank. On the opposite bank, I could see the gray chimney of what looked like some kind of factory.

"You okay?" I heard a voice behind me. The sound of the cicadas receded into the distance. I turned around and saw the lace hem of a long white skirt. Under it were unpainted toenails peeking out of a pair of brown sandals. I looked up, hoping to find a face. Maybe it was the sun or how she was holding her parasol, but I couldn't see anything. "Um, I'm okay. I just fell in." "Do you want help?" She reached down with her free hand. Her wrist was thin. "No, I'm fine. I can manage." "Are you sure?" She sounded like she was probably older—older than me, at least. I summoned my strength and tried again, failing miserably. It was deeper than I'd thought. Chunks of soft earth tumbled down into the hole. I thought I heard something scuttle by my feet, maybe a small animal that had popped out of its own hole, then retreated in panic.

"You don't look fine to me." The woman squatted down and offered her hand again. Her parasol moved and I caught a glimpse of her face. She was wearing large sunglasses that covered everything except her smile. She had to be older than me, but was probably younger than my mom. I was embarrassed, but hardly had a choice. I took her hand. It felt cold. I thought I could see veins running through it. Was this woman really strong enough? She counted down. "Three, two, one . . ." Then she tugged. I twisted my body and managed to get a hip onto the grass. As soon as I did, I felt something sting my hand. The woman was smiling. "You alright?" "I'm okay," I said, looking at my left hand. There was dirt under my nails. Near the top of my ring finger was a small red beetle, biting into me. I quickly hid my hand from the woman and thanked her for helping me. Her long skirt was covered in grass and flecks of sand. Her hand was dirty, too. "Sorry about your skirt," I said. "Don't worry about it. What are you doing out here in this heat?" She angled her parasol to share the shade with me. Her makeup was carefully done. Behind her amber sunglasses, I could barely make out the shape of her eyes. They looked like they were deep-set.

Behind my back, I tried flicking the insect off my finger. "I was on my way to the convenience store when I saw this animal . . ." Before I could finish explaining, the woman held out her hand and said, "Here, let me take a look." I didn't see any way out of this, so I gave her my hand. The red bug still clung tightly to my finger. It wasn't an insect I'd ever seen before. It almost looked like a ladybug, but smaller and with no spots. It hurt. "Well, look at that." She dug a nail into the bug. I almost pulled my hand back, but she'd already crushed the beetle's head to pieces. She flicked the bits of shell caught under her nails into the air, then wrapped her finger around mine so tightly I thought she was going to break it. The rest of the beetle fell to the ground, leaving only a drop of clear liquid where it had been attached. "Sorry, did that hurt? There are still some parts of its jaw in there. We need to get those out . . . Okay. All better. I'm pretty sure it isn't poisonous, but you should probably disinfect this when you get home." "Uh, okay. Thanks, I will." "Hey, so . . ." she said, bringing her face closer to mine. I couldn't see a single drop of sweat on her.

"You're the bride, aren't you?" The bride? How was I supposed to answer that? Her eyes were blinking behind her sunglasses, but soon all I could see in her face was a distorted version of my own. "Mune-chan's bride? My family lives next to the Matsuuras. You know, next to them, on the other side. We're the Seras . . ." "I . . ." There was a large house two lots over from us, bigger than my in-laws', and I'd seen the name SERA on the nameplate out front. When we moved in, Tomiko told me not to bother introducing myself—not just to the Seras, but to any of our new neighbors. "Don't worry about making the rounds. I'll keep an eye out and let you know when the time is right. A lot of our neighbors work odd hours and the last thing you want is for word to get out that you've gone around to meet some people, but not others." "I'm sorry I haven't introduced myself, I'm—" Matsuura, wife of Muneaki, son of . . . But before I could say it, she cut in, waving her parasol slowly from side to side. "It's fine." It almost smelled like incense, powdery and sweet. "I know who you are. You moved in the day we had all that rain, didn't you? Had to be a tough move. Well, I guess a hot day like today wouldn't have been any better. And we needed the rain . . . Still, I'd rather not be out in this heat. My son hasn't come home yet, but he has to get a shot today." "A shot? A vaccination?" "Hehehe. In this heat, right? Anyway, you're not lost, are you? Do you know where you are?" I thought I saw something moving by my feet, but when I looked down it was gone. "Um, sure, I know where I am. The store's that way." "Right. You'd better stay on the path. Don't get too close to the river." Sera smiled. Her forehead and cheeks were snowy white—only her lips were light brown. "Just go that way."

"I will. So, um, are there lots of holes around here? I didn't see it—I just fell in." "I really couldn't tell you, but my son would know. He's always out here, playing by the river. Then he comes home covered in mud and bugs . . . I only came this way because

I thought I might find him here. It was the strangest thing. From where I was standing, all I could see was your head poking out of the ground. Right away, I thought, that has to be the bride . . ." She snickered. As she brought her hand up to her mouth, her wedding ring glimmered in the light. Why did she keep calling me "the bride"? No one had ever called me that before. When I was working, people always called me Matsuura. Then again, we'd just met. She could hardly call me "Asa" the way Tomiko does. She definitely couldn't call me "Matsuura." For her, that had to mean Tomiko. Even my husband couldn't be "Matsuura" in her eyes. I guess that would make me "the bride." I'd been the bride for a while and simply hadn't realized it. Sera turned and looked up the slope. A sweet smell filled my nose again. I noticed that the inside of her white parasol was yellowed with age.

"Sorry I took up so much of your time . . . I truly appreciate the help." "Oh, it's no problem. I'm glad we had the chance to talk. Well, I'd better get going." I bowed and thanked her again. As she started to walk away, she smiled even wider and said, "Matsuura's a real good one, isn't she? You must be happy to have her as your mother-in-law." I nodded. "Oh, I am." "I can imagine. You're a lucky girl. Well, see you around." With that, Sera walked slowly up the bank, bits of grass still clinging to her skirt.

Once I was alone again, I knelt down and looked into the hole. It was too dark to see the bottom. I looked around the riverbank. The animal was nowhere to be seen. The river was moving in the direction of the store. The cicadas crescendoed again. What was that animal? I should have asked Sera about it. I couldn't even tell if it was wild or some kind of pet. It didn't really seem like either. I thought I saw a boy pop his head out of the grass, then duck back down. When I looked up again, Sera and her parasol were just a white dot in the distance. I watched as she disappeared around a curve in the path. I walked out of the grass, followed the path for a little while, then crossed a bridge.

As soon as I was across, I found the convenience store, just where I thought it would be.

There were children inside. Some were sitting on the floor looking at manga, some were rearranging the Q-tips and disposable razors, and others were sticking their faces in the ice cream freezer. As I maneuvered between them to reach the register, I pulled out Tomiko's pay slip. An older woman with brownish hair, the only employee in the store, took out the store seal, stamped the slip, then asked for 74,000 yen. I took the bills out of Tomiko's envelope: five 10,000-yen bills, nothing else. 50,000 yen? I immediately opened my own wallet, but I only had another 10,000-yen bill. "Did you say ... 74,000?" "Uh-huh," the clerk said, showing me the number on the slip. She was right. The money was going to some company I'd never heard of, but it sounded like it had to be some sort of health food company. "I'm sorry ... I don't have ..." The clerk gave me an annoyed look, having already stamped the slip with today's date. She had to be as old as Tomiko, maybe a little older. The wrinkles on her neck stood out against her brightly colored uniform. "I don't have the cash. I'll need to use the ATM." She tilted her head quizzically and asked, "You mean right now?" "You have a machine, don't you?" She smiled a little. "Right there, next to the copier." It was the usual setup, the same as every 7-Eleven in the city. I pulled out my card and walked toward the machine, but found my path was blocked. In front of the shrink-wrapped manga, a battalion of children obstructed the aisle. They looked like they were probably in the first or second grade, but could've been younger than that. They were completely absorbed in their comics, not even noticing me. I don't know if it was the radio or not, but there was music playing in the store. It was the latest pop music. I had no idea who the singer was, if they were male or female, but it sounded like they were twelve. "Excuse me," I said to the children. They didn't move a muscle. I looked to the clerk for help, but she was too busy to notice. "Hello?" Other than their fingers flipping the pages, the children were perfectly still. Their mouths were open, their eyes never left the comics. "Kids . . ." I heard a man say. "See this lady standing here? You're in her way. She's trying to get to that machine so she can get money. Give her some room, okay?"

They quickly turned to look up at me. The corners of their mouths were white with powder. It smelled sour-sweet. I turned to see where the voice had come from. It belonged to a middle-aged man in a white open-collar shirt and black slacks. He was thin, and a little on the short side. He had his hands on his hips, and was holding a comic book that was as thick as a dictionary. Only his face was turned toward me. "Are we in the way?" "Are we in her way?" the children asked in tinny voices as they stood up and swarmed around me. They were all wearing shorts and jumper skirts. A few of them had sandals—more like clogs, really—and their toenails were black with dirt. "Sorry." Keeping an eye on both the children and the man, I made my way to the ATM. I slid my card into the slot and started typing in my PIN, but the children were right there, watching closely. The guard over the keypad, for preventing others from seeing you put in your code, has no effect on grade schoolers. They're too short. One of them nestled up under my arm as if we were family. From the way he was looking at the screen on the ATM, you would have thought it was a TV showing some cartoon. "Sorry, can you stop looking, please?" "Whyyy?" Come on, don't act like you don't know how ATMs work. Then again, these kids were so young that maybe they really didn't. Every bit of attention that the children had given to the manga was now directed at me, so I had to use my free hand to cover the keypad as I finished typing in my code. I pressed WITHDRAW, typed in "24,000," then pressed ENTER. As I grabbed the bills from the machine, it seemed pointless to put them in my wallet, so I walked over to the register, money in hand, when one of the little children screeched. "Sensei!" Sensei? The man in the white shirt nodded, then smiled at me with all his teeth. I nodded back without thinking. "Sensei! This lady's got a lot of money. That's a 10,000-yen bill!" The other children broke into laughter. "That's a lot of money!" The man smiled wryly and said, "It sure is, but we don't talk about things like that in public, do we? So shush . . ." "Shush?" "Shush!" "Shush!!" The children were practically bouncing off the walls, squealing. The man started laughing and so did the children. I did the same. Only the clerk was expressionless as she grabbed the bills from my hand. She counted them once, then held them up and counted again for my benefit. Well, it didn't look like I'd have any change for ice cream. I didn't have much money saved up. I was unemployed now, so dipping into my savings was the last thing I wanted to do, but what choice did I have? What was going on with Tomiko? She'd always been on top of things.

I nodded at the man the children called Sensei and left the store. As soon as I stepped outside, the cicadas and the heat descended upon me. On the other side of the glass, the children in the store were waving at me with white palms. I waved back, then followed the river home. On the way back, I didn't see anyone. Every now and then, I'd look down to the riverbank, but didn't see the animal. I saw no life at all. The river was so stagnant it looked like it was made of gelatin. When I got to Tomiko's house, Grandpa was outside, still watering. Together with the copy of the stamped slip, I left a note on the desk saying there wasn't enough money and that I'd covered the difference. After some thought, I decided against writing exactly how much I'd paid. I had to believe that Tomiko would remember how much she'd left in the envelope.

That night, when Tomiko got home, she came over to apologize. She gave me 4,000 yen. Stock-still, I stared at the four crisp bills as she said, "I must have really been out of it. I'm so embarrassed. You really helped me out, though. I know you couldn't get any ice cream, so ... I brought these," she said, handing me two Popsicles, each as thick as a couple of fingers. As I took the Popsicles, Tomiko shrugged—although I wasn't sure why. "Save one for Muneaki, okay? This was all they had in stock. But you'll like them, I promise. They're from the co-op. The soda-flavored one is really good. It really fizzes when you bite into it. Oh, they deliver, too. Next time, I'll bring the catalog for you. The co-op catalog." She kept talking about the co-op and their frozen desserts, but I didn't know how to tell her that her 4,000 yen wasn't even close. I thanked her for the Popsicles. Maybe she had no idea how much money she'd actually put in the envelope ... Or maybe someone had come in when the door was unlocked and skimmed some of the money. Maybe it was Grandpa. Who knows. Whatever the case, we were living rent-free. And it was only 20,000 yen. I had to let it slide. I put the Popsicles in the freezer and waited for my husband to come home. When he got back, it was after midnight. Since our move, that was more or less normal.

"I saw a weird black animal today," I said as I set out dinner for my husband. He looked up from his phone and said, "Oh yeah?" His hair was wet from the shower he'd taken. He probably didn't bother drying it—or maybe he was just sweaty. The back of the blue shirt he always wore to sleep was so wet it looked almost black. As soon as he sent me a text saying he'd be home in a few minutes, I turned on the AC. For me, the room was like an icebox, but maybe my husband was still hot. He put down his phone and picked up his chopsticks. He inhaled his rice, then chased it down with a mouthful of miso soup. I'd made the soup while he was in the shower. "It had black fur and was probably this big." I held up my hands so he could see. "Was it a stray dog or something?" he asked, finishing his mugicha. "I'm pretty sure it wasn't a dog." "Maybe it was a raccoon. I remember hearing there are a lot of raccoons around here, or at least there used to be." "I'm pretty sure it wasn't a raccoon." "How do you know?" "I know what a raccoon looks like." I filled my husband's cup with mugicha. He used his chopsticks to lift the omelet onto his rice, brought the omelet up to his mouth, then reached for his mugicha. Now there was ketchup on his rice. "Whatever it was, I followed it into the grass—and I fell into a hole." "A hole?" He reached for the pickled cucumber and tossed it in his mouth with the ketchup-covered rice, then finally chewed a few times. I listened to the crunch. I'd already eaten my dinner. I didn't make an omelet for myself. I just had some meat and a single egg—sunny-side up—over a bowl of rice. Before we moved, my husband never came home this late. I was always working overtime, too, so we'd eat together—even if it was some reheated curry or stir-fry. I never had the energy to go to the supermarket after a long day at work, so we hardly ever had vegetables. We had a few frozen things that we could heat up—fried rice and things like that. Now I never bought anything premade. I made our meals from scratch. This was far better for us, both financially and nutritionally. At the same time, I'd pass out from hunger if I tried to wait for my husband to come home. It's not like eating together meant that much to me, but when you make dinner twice a day, one of those meals is going to lack heart. Miso soup is best when it's fresh. Anything pickled is going to get soggy eventually. Fried food mutates into something else when you reheat it. "How deep was it?" "Up to my chest. A little deeper, maybe." "No way." You can't survive on boiled pork or meat and potatoes.

Maybe there wasn't anywhere for him to eat around his office. Or maybe he was eating at home for me—for my benefit. Either way, it didn't matter how late it was when my husband came home. That's when he ate. For the most part, I was happy with this arrangement. I think I'd feel guilty if he ever said, "I don't need dinner tonight." I'd probably feel like something was missing, like I wasn't holding up my end of the bargain. Not long after the move, I asked him if he ever got hungry working that late without dinner. He told me there were snacks at work—nothing substantial, but enough to hold him over. I asked him where the snacks came from, who brought them. He said no one brought them—they were always there, in the office, free for the taking. I imagined my husband, working overtime and digging into a giant bag of chocolates or maybe some manju from a client. The thought of it was too much to bear. "It's usually just Kameda Crisps, but sometimes we have dried squid." "Squid?" "Yeah, on sticks. Skewered. They're just there in the break room—who knows why. Maybe there were a bunch left over from some party or something." Every workplace has its own logic. At my old job, no one saw squid as an office snack. There's no way anyone would have gotten away with it. Anyone who dared to eat Kameda Crisps would've faced an even worse fate. Why would anyone make that kind of noise when everybody else is trying to finish up for the day? If someone did that at my old job, they'd never hear the end of it. I thought I knew what kind of place my husband's office was, but maybe I knew less than I realized. It's not like I didn't care. He didn't know that much about my old job, either. Whenever someone asked me what my husband did, I had my answer ready. Still, I have to admit, I didn't have a firm grasp on how his business turned a profit, or what role my husband really played in it.

My husband kept an eye on the news as he swallowed the rest of his dinner with inhuman speed. "Sounds dangerous. You'd better watch out for holes. Stay away from those animals, too, whatever they are." "But I'd never seen it before." "I bet it was just some weird breed of dog. Dogs come in all shapes and sizes. Or maybe it was a weasel. Seriously, raccoons don't look the way they do in comics. I've never seen one in real life either." But it wasn't a dog, and it wasn't a weasel or a raccoon. Not that I knew what it was. Regardless, I didn't have any hard evidence to prove him wrong, so I just nodded while his attention returned to the phone in his hand. I watched as his fingers sped across the screen. There was a small, hard lump on my finger where the bug had bitten me. It felt hot. I put a bandage over it and went to sleep.

IT WAS ANOTHER TWO MONTHS BEFORE IT REALLY RAINED. We'd had brief showers and a little drizzle, but nothing significant. Every day was unbearably hot. If it hadn't rained so heavily on the day of our move, we probably would have been in a drought. Or maybe the local river and reservoir simply had that much water. The next time it really rained, I went around the house, closing all the windows so the water wouldn't get in. Looking through the upstairs window on the west side of the house, I could see Grandpa. He was out in the garden wearing a raincoat. I stood there for a little while, watching him, trying to understand what I was seeing. There he was, hose in hand, watering the plants in the middle of the rain.

In the gray downpour, Grandpa was maneuvering the hose, its green body wriggling in the dark. I wondered if I should go down and say something. But what could I say? Even if I knew what to say, I wasn't sure he'd be able to hear me. I drew the curtain and headed downstairs. Looking out the garden window, I saw mounds of exposed earth turning muddy in the rain. On the other side of the concrete-block wall, I could still see Grandpa. I closed that curtain, too, then went to the couch and opened up a magazine to look for jobs—not even expecting to find anything reasonable within walking distance. There were a handful of listings for pharmacists and nurses. I found some for truck drivers, too, but I couldn't drive stick. No office jobs. I couldn't even find a part-time job working as a cashier. I got up and went to the kitchen. I watched the rain from the small window—the only one where I couldn't see Grandpa. I had a view of the street. There wasn't anyone walking or driving past. Every other window in the house was shut, but the sound of rain filled the house. Cicadas are quiet when it rains. It got me thinking: What would a cicada do if it emerged from the earth and there was nothing but rain for days on end? Would it just die without ever making a sound? The doorbell rang. I jumped. When I opened the door, I saw Sera. The rain behind her was falling harder than before.

"It's really pouring, isn't it? I suppose we needed it, but this is a lot of rain." She folded her black umbrella. It was full-size, the kind that businessmen carry. I invited her in. She took one step inside, then asked, "Are you sure you don't mind? My shoes are soaked." "No, of course not. Come in. And thanks again for the other day." She propped her umbrella against the wall by the door. Sera said her shoes were soaked, but they looked more or less dry to me. She had a cotton bag over her shoulder, but that wasn't wet either. "Oh, it was nothing. How's Mune-chan? It looks like he doesn't get home until pretty late at night. He's almost like the man of the house, isn't he?" It took me a second to process, but "man of the house" had to mean my husband's father, my father-in-law. I had to remind myself how, in her mind, the Matsuuras could only be my husband's parents. Muneaki was "Mune-chan" and I was his "bride."

We were standing in the entryway. What was I supposed to do? Ask her to come in and sit down? Offer her some tea? Would mugicha be okay? Should I give her something to snack on? The house was hardly a mess—it was as clean as it could be—but Sera didn't seem at all interested in coming inside. "He gets in after midnight a lot, doesn't he? Is his office far from here?" "It's a thirty-minute drive, but he's still getting settled. It seems like they're keeping him really busy," I said. Sera put her hand up to her lips and mouthed the word *wow*. "Amazing. Mune-chan's a real working man now. Scary how time flies, isn't it? Ten, twenty years, in the blink of an eye." It looked like she might have been wearing the same outfit as last time, when she helped me out of the hole. White blouse and skirt. Of course she wasn't wearing sunglasses this time. I could really see her eyes. They were a little sunken and tired-looking, but her eyelashes were long and beautiful. She must've been a real beauty in her day. "What about you? Are you working? What are you doing to pass the time?" I glanced at my feet. I'd painted my toenails the other day when I had nothing else to do. They didn't stand out—I didn't have any bright colors like red or blue. I only had a couple of subtler shades: beige and light pink. You could hardly tell I'd done them. I felt a little embarrassed standing there barefoot, but realized it would have seemed weirder if I had been walking around my own house in socks in the middle of the summer. "I'm not working right now. I'm looking, but I don't have a car, so it isn't easy getting around." Sera nodded sympathetically. She had the same sweet smell as before. "I know what you mean. You need a car around here, don't you? I don't even have a license. I can barely ride a bicycle, so I need to rely on my husband wherever I go. I can walk if it's close enough, or take a bus—but they don't come here very often. I'm from the city originally. About twenty years ago I got married and came here. A little longer, maybe. Back then, this place was literally the middle of nowhere. I kept asking myself how I'd ended up way out here. In those days, even getting a taxi was hard. If you called the company, they'd tell you it'd take thirty minutes for the car to come. It's a whole lot better now, but it's still not like the city, is it? Especially when it comes to finding a job." "Well, I could try finding something I could reach by bus or train, but . . ." "Free time is a real problem, isn't it? Who needs a summer vacation that never ends—am I right?" As I nodded, I thought I could feel tears welling in my eyes.

I didn't actually hate having nothing to do. I'm sure if I were seriously looking I'd be able to find a place to work that I could get to in under an hour by bus or an hour or two by bike. If I were truly desperate, I could dip into my savings and buy a moped, which would allow me to cast a wider net. In short, I couldn't really say there were no jobs to be had. I just wasn't putting much effort into it. It's not like I was hung up on finding some high-paying gig as a permanent employee. I didn't feel the need to work. I couldn't see the benefit. I didn't need it. I could live without working. My husband's salary had improved, at least a little, and his commute was covered. Plus, he was collecting overtime on a nightly basis. On the other end of things, we were spending less money than ever before. We weren't buying convenience-store food or frozen dinners. The local supermarket was a whole lot cheaper than the one in the city. At our old place, I would have to wait every week for the milk to go on sale, but out here it was cheaper than that sale price all week long. It was better milk, too. We could afford to stock up on vegetables here. But more than anything else, we were getting by without paying any rent. My old job in the city paid just enough to cover our rent—and I could pitch in with some of the expenses as long as I was working overtime. Compared to a permanent employee, I probably had it easy there, but that job came with a fair amount of hard work and responsibility. I put myself through that pain so that we'd have a place to stay, but now, through the good graces of my mother-in-law, there was no need to worry about any of that. Endless summer vacation. But it didn't feel right. My husband was working late every night while I was at home, on my own, with all the time in the world? I had to work. Even if I couldn't find a job, I had to do something. My body was getting heavier with every passing day. Not that I was gaining weight. On the contrary. But I could barely move. It was as if every muscle and joint, every cell in my body, was stuck. Putting it that way makes it sound like I was blaming my body, like it was beyond my control. I was slipping, and it was completely my fault. It was only a matter of time before Grandpa or Muneaki or Tomiko tore me apart for being so lazy. And they'd be right. Except—would any of them ever say something like that to my face?

Sera continued, indifferent to my silence. "What can you do for fun, right? I'd tell you to come over and talk to me whenever you want, but I'm a little older than you, and I have a child to look after. If you had a child, you'd have your hands full, believe me ... But why not have a kid? Can you?" I sighed. I wanted to answer, but I realized my voice wasn't coming, so I tilted my head to the side and tried to smile. Children. Having a child would change things, but it wasn't exactly the change I was looking for. Besides, was this really the right environment for raising a kid? The buzz of cicadas, the splash of Grandpa's hose, Tomiko's weird doggy slippers, and my husband and his phone. Just imagining myself breastfeeding a baby in the middle of all that was enough to depress me. I didn't exactly hate the idea of having a child. Maybe it could make me happy. Maybe it was the best thing to do if I wasn't going to go back to work. Sera looked me in the eye, smiled, and said, "I understand. I was older when I had my son. I had to stay at the hospital. We were there for a while, too. In the end, my baby was fine, but they had him in an incubator for a long time ... I couldn't do anything but watch. It was so hard. It wasn't easy for my husband or his mother, either. I can't even imagine what my son was going through. He's five now. I'm sure you can hear him sometimes. He's not as mature as the other kids his age, not that there's anything wrong with that. I suppose that's half nurture, but it's also half nature. Anyway, you're still so young—with so much to look forward to.

I'm sure Matsuura-san has told you some stories. I know Taka-chan wasn't easy for her . . ." "Taka-chan?" I asked back. Sera clicked her tongue, then contorted her face in apology. "No, wait, hold on. Did I say Taka? I got mixed up. Sometimes I have these thoughts in my brain, but the words that come out are completely different. You're too young to know what I mean, but sometimes I just space out . . ." "No, no. I understand." I nodded. I was pretty sure I was more spaced out than she was. If I were fully awake, I wouldn't know how I'd get through each day. Sera touched her lips with her fingers. Unlike the other day, they were glistening red. "Mune-chan, Mune-chan. I remember when he was only a baby. To think of him, all grown up, going off to work, then coming home with a bride of his own . . . Matsuura-san must be overjoyed. It's a lot sometimes, I know, but I'm sure you'll do fine. What am I saying? Just listen to me go. That's not why I came by. I wanted to give you these. No one in my family likes them, but what about you?"

She reached inside her cotton bag and pulled out a smaller plastic bag—inside were a few green things shaped like spindles. "What are they?" "Myoga. You've never had myoga?" She was looking at me like I was an alien. "No—I have." I'd just never bought any. Besides, they didn't look anything like the little reddish things I was used to seeing piled up at the supermarket—these were large and bright green. Toward the end, they exploded into large, unwieldy fingers. "Um, this is what goes on hiyayakko, right?" "Yeah, exactly. You chop it up. It goes well with tofu and noodles. You can pickle it in sweet vinegar, too. We're not even trying to grow myoga anymore, but they still pop up in our garden every year. Tons of them. I used to eat myoga all the time, but no one else in my family likes it, so it didn't make any sense to keep growing it . . . But it's great with vinegared miso dressing. Throw a little sugar in, too, to sweeten things up," Sera said, dangling the bag between us. I thanked her and took it. I could feel its coolness through the plastic. Clutching one of the plants, I found it surprisingly hard. It was covered in fine hair and didn't feel like any leaf or stem or fruit I knew. "What part of the plant is this?" Sera tilted her head in response. I could see more plastic bags full of greens. She must've been going around the neighborhood, handing out myoga. I guess she really did have tons of the stuff. "This is the whole thing. They shoot out of the ground, just like this. If you let them grow, white flowers come out of the tips. It's pretty. They look a little like orchids. You can eat the flowers, too." Looking inside the bag, I could smell rain mixed with earth.

Once Sera left, I put the bag of myoga in the fridge, then went to the living room window. I could see Grandpa outside, crouching down. There was something black at his feet. It looked like he was petting a cat. Whatever he was doing, it had to be better than running the hose in the middle of the pouring rain.

"What's in this?" "Myoga." "Myoga?" my husband asked, spitting out the vinegared miso he'd had in his mouth. Looking around online, I found that myoga buds are also called "spikes." I took Sera's advice and used them in a dressing. When I tried it, I thought it was pretty good. It had a unique texture to it, and I'd never smelled anything quite like it—it would probably go well with sake. "Myoga?" my husband said again after he'd washed his mouth out with mugicha. "You don't have to eat it if you don't want." "Sorry, I don't think I can handle it. What made you buy myoga? Was it on sale or something?" "No, Sera-san came over and gave me a bag." "Sera-san?" My husband sounded like he had no idea who I was talking about. I ate the myoga I'd dished out for him. Tasted fine to me. It was nice and light. I could even smell the rain mixed with the vinegar and miso. "The woman on the other side of my parents' house?" "Yeah." "Huh. I didn't realize you knew her." "Well, I'd hardly say I know her." My husband's free hand glided over the surface of his phone while he snacked on other things. I didn't know who he was writing to, but I'm sure he was typing something like "I can't believe my wife just tried to make me eat the world's shittiest myoga." I sighed. "What?" He looked up at me. "Nothing," I said, shaking my head.

I WOKE UP TO THE LOUD CRIES OF THE CICADAS. WHEN we went to sleep the night before, it was still raining. It was so muggy that we shut the windows and left the AC running when we went to bed. Why were the cicadas so loud? I looked at the clock. My alarm wasn't set to go off for a long time. My husband was sleeping next to me, turned the other way. His shirt had slid halfway up his back, revealing a few white spots that looked like pimples. I crawled out of bed and looked out the window. It was hard to believe it had been raining the night before. The weather was beautiful now. Grandpa was out in the garden, watering the plants. What I thought had been cicadas was the sound of the hose. I felt as if my knees were about to give. Grandpa wore the same outfit as always: a straw hat, gray long-sleeve shirt, and pants. I suppose the best way to water the garden is to get started before the sun rises, but how long was he going to be out there? It wasn't exactly the biggest yard. Where was all the water going?

After I saw my husband off to work, I went next door. It had been several hours since I'd looked out the window and seen Grandpa running the hose, but—of course—he was still there. Tomiko was already gone. From the gate, I called out in a fairly loud voice, "Grandpa! How long are you going to be gardening?" He gave no response, so I took a few steps in his direction.

Once he saw me, he turned toward me with a hand in the air, baring his teeth in a smile. Now that he was looking right at me, I tried again. "How's the garden?" As I spoke, his smile shrank for a moment, then grew back. Now he was really showing his teeth. It wasn't even eight yet, but it was already scorching out. I moved closer to the house, into the shade, and watched Grandpa as he got back to the task at hand. His lips formed a tight circle, as if he were whistling, but he wasn't making a sound. I looked at the plants around the garden. There were morning glories in red and dark blue, the flowers clinging to their own leaves. There were giant red cannas and sunflowers the color of molasses. Among the wild weeds and yellowing pots, I could see dark purple clumps of wood sorrels and a few light red plants I couldn't name, but it was clearly some sort of garden species. Everything seemed to strike a strange balance—maybe because it was summer? The scene hummed with a green vitality that flowed through the windless garden. A grasshopper leapt onto a leaf, then flew away, the stalk trembling in its wake.

In the bushes beyond the sun, a black shadow blinked. A pair of bright yellow circles closed, then opened again. A large, round frog. Close to it was a single dahlia, swarming with yellow aphids moving sluggishly up and down the long stem. The aphids had eyes. They were only black dots, no bigger than the tip of a needle, but I could see them with terrible clarity. They looked so large that I thought something had to be wrong with my own eyes. The flowers were past their peak. Their petals were curling up, changing color. It looked like the frog was about to feed on the aphids. I waited for it to unleash its pink tongue and snap up the unsuspecting insects. The dahlia collapsed from the root. A blast of water had knocked it over. Grandpa—whistling soundlessly—was flooding the garden around him, leaving the dahlia on its side before moving on to the bush where the frog had been. A single cicada shook its abdomen clumsily as it began to cross the garden, stopping to release a stream of clear fluid, then began to buzz. *Chiii, chit, chit.* Grandpa looked at me as if he had just remembered I was there, then returned to his usual pose. "Grandpa ... the water ..." He nodded and held his hand up at what was probably a right angle to his body, but his whole body was tilted to one side. Just when I thought he couldn't grin any wider, he did. He couldn't hear a word I said. Beneath his giant hat, his teeth were shining. His eyes and nose were hidden in shadow. Only his mouth—a rigid smile—was clear to me. It didn't even look like a smile to me anymore, but I had to believe that it was. As I looked at the garden, now reduced to mud, I saw a black animal coming toward the gate. Its face was strangely long and pointy. Its yellow eyes were trained on me. A few stray drops from Grandpa's hose splashed across its snout. The animal jumped a little, then quickened its steps. I looked at Grandpa. He must have noticed the animal, but carried on just the same. He continued to spray water all around, his lips puckered in a tight circle, producing more spit than sound. The animal came closer, then shook its body. No water flew off of it. It wasn't very wet. It couldn't be the same animal as before. Its fur looked a little softer, its tail a little shorter. The animal swaggered across the garden, behind Tomiko's house, then disappeared around the corner. Grandpa was looking elsewhere, his lips pursed as he turned the water up. The green hose shook behind him and the water shot through the garden. I went after the animal.

Between Tomiko's house and the Seras' was a concrete-block wall—like the one between Tomiko's house and ours, but maybe a foot or two taller. There was a break in the blocks just large enough for a person to squeeze through. It was dark, hidden in shadow. In the darkness, I could make out hind legs and a short tail, only for a moment, before the animal vanished. I went after it. Thick layers of spiderwebs hung between the concrete wall and the house. They got all over my face and in my mouth. I tried to peel the webs from my face. On the back wall of the house were dried clumps of earth drooping down. They could have been smears of mud left behind by a child—or maybe some sort of insect nest. A few of the concrete blocks had fan-shaped holes in them. Through the openings, I could see the yard next door—the Seras' yard. The grass was as green as could be, and covered with bright red and yellow objects. Maybe they were her son's toys? I imagined Sera in her white skirt, watering the lawn. Nothing like Grandpa in his muddy boots. What I envisioned was a happier scene—a child playing gleefully at her feet. At the edge of Tomiko's house, a small space appeared. There was no animal. Instead I saw a middle-aged man. The cries of the cicadas stopped.

The man was crouching down, his arm shoved through one of the open blocks. I froze. He looked right at me. He was thin, with black hair, wearing a white open-collar shirt. I'd seen him before, at the 7-Eleven. It was the man the children had called Sensei. "Hello there!" the man shouted. I gulped. Behind the man, I saw a small building—some sort of prefabricated shack. "And who might you be?" he asked loudly, a smile on his face.

If this man were an intruder and I had to call for help, the Seras' house was probably closer than Grandpa. Besides, Grandpa wouldn't even hear me. As I wondered whether Sera was home, I tried my best to answer him: "I live, in the house, next, next to this one ..." "Right, right. The bride. When you say 'next to,' you mean on the opposite side, right? You moved in just a little while ago ..." He had a friendly way of talking. He didn't seem at all dangerous or threatening, but I couldn't be sure. "I'm the older son. Mune's older brother. A lot older, really." "Huh?" My mouth was hanging open. The man continued. "I suppose that makes me your ... what? What's that called again? It's on the tip of my tongue, I swear. I'm your husband's brother, and that makes me your, uh, your brother, brother-in . . . brother-in-what . . ." "Law?" "Right! Your brother-in-law."

"My brother-in-law?" I asked. As I did, I shrank back, not so much that he would have noticed. My husband's brother? "Right, right. Your brother-in-law. That's who I am. Nice to meet you." All of a sudden, I could smell something like freshly mown grass—as though something inside me had cleared. The man looked up at me, showing his teeth in a smile. But I thought my husband was an only child. No one had ever said otherwise. "From the look on your face, I'm guessing no one told you about me. I suppose that's understandable. It's a bit of a tragic situation, really. You see this shack—this shed?" the man asked, pointing to the cream-colored structure behind him. It reminded me of the sort of temporary housing that you see in disaster zones. It was small, but had two stories. Same as Tomiko's house, the walls were covered in clumps of dry earth—higher up, a few of them had holes in them. The building had a brown sliding door with a small keyhole to one side. "This is where I've lived for the last twenty years." "Twenty years?" I asked. "I know, it's a long time, right? Twenty years ago, you couldn't have been more than a guppy. Anyway, I was big by then. I stopped going to school, dragged my bed into the shed, and started living on my own. My parents probably thought I was going through some kind of phase, but I was hell-bent on getting out, even when I was just a boy. But I never had the chance. You gotta have a place, right? Right around that time, we got the shed back here. A beautiful two-story shed. We'd been farming and needed more space to store some gear. Then I hijacked the shed! Under the cover of night, of course. It was a real coup, let me tell you. And that's the way it's been for twenty years. Haven't put in an honest day's work since. I'm a real good-for-nothing!" the man shouted in excitement. When he finally stopped to take a breath, he made a serious face, then whispered, "I guess that makes me what they call a hikikomori—a shut-in."

His hair was dark, so he didn't look much older than my husband—not that I had any clue how old he was. His thin lips were bright red. Under his open-collar shirt, I could see a tank top. They both looked pretty clean. His slacks were dark navy, or maybe black. They looked like the sort of pants middle schoolers wear with their summer uniforms. Maybe they were. The more I thought about it, his outfit really was strange. His shoes were black leather, shining like they'd just been polished. He still had his arm shoved into the wall. There didn't seem to be anything on the other side. Then it hit me how cool the air was—nothing like the heat out front. In the shade of the house, the air was cold. Moss grew toward the bottom of the wall and on the ground below. Where there was no moss, it was black. It didn't look muddy, but it was probably damp. The narrow walkway was dry. It looked like it forked off at some point. The ground wasn't wet like the garden out front. Here there was balance—moist air seemed to rise up from the earth itself, cool and damp. The air had that same grassy smell, almost like fresh tatami, and maybe a little incense. Growing on the ground were clusters of dark violet with white flowers on top. "That's bishop's weed. Granny used to make tea with it. Mom can't stand the smell . . . Personally, I love it, because I was always Granny's boy. Still, Mom never drank Granny's tea. She didn't want me touching it either. But now look. It's everywhere. Hey, what if you took some home and made tea? I bet it'd be really good if you dried it out . . ." "Um . . ." Images flashed in my mind, one after another. Grandma's photograph from the altar room. Then Tomiko, Muneaki, and—for whatever reason—the Sera woman. Last of all, I saw Grandpa, smiling as always. My husband's brother . . . My brother-in-law? How did everyone know so much about me when I knew nothing about them?

"By the way, it's probably best if you don't tell anyone we met.

Not Mom, definitely not Muneaki. They wouldn't be happy about it. I don't care what they think of me, but it'd be unfortunate if they took that out on you. Of course, it's your choice to make ..." Tomiko's face came back to me, clear as day. Then, breaking off from that image, my husband's face resurfaced. There was no reason to think I knew the truth about everything. Sure, no one dragged me here against my will. I wasn't unhappy, I wasn't dissatisfied. I knew what I was getting into. But that doesn't mean I knew everything. Why couldn't I hear the cicadas back here? "Are you really Muneaki's brother?" I asked in a voice I didn't recognize. "Sure am. Can't blame you for asking, but you're *just asking*, right? I mean, if you didn't believe me, if you thought I was suspicious, you would have already run off to alert the authorities. Then again, I guess it's hard to trust your eyes on this. After all, Muneaki and I look nothing alike. I don't really look like my mom or my dad either. I can't imagine you've seen much of him anyway. He's got to be as busy as ever. I haven't seen his car for a little while, but he's still kicking, isn't he? Last I saw, he'd just traded in for a silver Mazda. It's always Mazdas with my old man. Always has been. The last one I ever got in was his Mazda Familiar. Pretty sure they stopped making those years ago. Leaving the house around dawn, coming home late at night ... It's a real sickness. Even on days off, he's always going fishing or golfing. Otherwise he can't relax. When we were kids and we had time off from school, he'd take us somewhere to camp or have a barbecue. I guess it isn't just looks. Even our personalities are total opposites. But don't you think I look like Gramps? People always said so, ever since I was a baby. Granny was always saying it. Anyway, I bet I'll go bald within ten years. Then you'll have all the proof you'll need." Something about him was strange, but he seemed completely harmless. Maybe it was his smile, which really did look a lot like Grandpa's. His long teeth grew thicker as they moved away from the gums. His broad forehead reminded me of Grandpa's, too. Grandpa was always wearing his big straw hat, but I could tell that there was something similar about the shape of their heads.

The man who said he was my brother-in-law licked his bottom lip, then the top one, before yanking his arm out of the wall. I heard a small voice and, for a second, saw a tiny, red hand on the other side of the hole. When he saw me spring back, the man stood up and looked me in the eye. "Don't worry, it's just a game we like to play, me and the shrimp. Wait, no, I can't call him that. He'll bite my head off. He's a proud one, my buddy next door. Anyway, it was time for us to call it quits. It's blazing hot out. Just look . . ." He held his hands out for me to see. The one that had been in the wall was bright red, but the other was weirdly pale. I bet his body temperature runs low. It's the same for my husband, even though he's always complaining about the heat. Sometimes in the morning, he's so cold I almost wonder if he's dead. Maybe it's something they have in common—as brothers. I tried looking for the kid on the other side of the wall, but didn't see anyone. I didn't know if he'd run off or was just hiding, but I could sense some kind of heat, like there was something there. The man shrugged. "Poor guy. He's always on his own. His old lady's no spring chicken and his dad's always tied up at work. Kindergarten wasn't any good for him either, so they had to pull him. Real shame. He'd honestly be better off with me looking after him." The Seras' house was quiet. The bright yellow objects on the lawn were a pair of children's rubber boots. "Okay now." The man flipped his hand over, looked at his fingernails, then brushed his fingers against the sides of his shirt.

"Tell me about you. Who are you? How'd you find yourself here?" "Huh? Uh, there was this black animal just now . . ." "Oh, him?" The man was pointing at a round hole in the ground covered with a metal grill. "He's in there." "Huh? The animal's in there?" I craned my neck, but all I could see were long white objects in the darkness. "What are those white . . ." "They're fangs. I know it's cute how they curl, but they're really sharp. They're practically weapons." "Fangs?" That animal had fangs? Then again, how would I know? I didn't know anything. "What kind of animal is it?" The man shrugged again. "Beats me." I could see the outline of his bony shoulders inside his baggy shirt. "But I know all about him. If you want to know about his behavior or personality, I could tell you anything you'd want to know. Of course, all that would be based on my personal observations." "Personal observations?" The man broke into a grin. "This hole is our old well. The house was built over a lot of water. The bottom of the well's been filled in with concrete, so you can't get any water out of it now . . . But anyway, he seems to like it down there. I guess this hole is a lot like the ones he digs. When he crawls down there, he'll go to sleep. It's not like he's here every night, but he's definitely down there a few nights a week. Whenever I see him down there, I cover the thing up," he said, kicking at the metal. A centipede crawling across the grating slipped under in a panic. "Then he's trapped. You can't get the lid off unless you put a finger in there and lift, but this guy's a smart one. He can push it open with his fangs . . . If you're wondering why I bother putting the cover on when he's only going to get out again, I'm afraid I don't have a good answer for you. I guess I'm just hoping he'll eventually decide to settle down and stay put. He digs his own holes, but when he finds an open one, he gets lazy and crawls inside." I had my eye on the white objects on the other side of the metal, but they weren't moving. They didn't look like fangs—or any other animal part—at least not any part that belonged to the creature I'd seen out front. Whatever I was staring at, I had the feeling it had been there for a long time. The bright sunlight didn't reach inside the hole. I tried to find the animal's eyes, but couldn't. Over time, even the fangs disappeared in the darkness. "Have you ever looked it up?"

"Looked it up?" "You know, on the Internet. Searched for 'black animal,' 'fangs' . . ." "What for?" he asked, his head tilted to the side. "I've never used the Internet. I don't have a computer. No television either. I think I get how it works, though. I've seen it in comics. What about you? Do you have a device like that?" I nodded. "Huh. So, what does that get you? Looking it up." "You can learn about the animal. Its name, important facts . . ." But, as I spoke, I realized the search wouldn't yield any results. With generic keywords like that, you'd probably get a million hits—none of which would have anything to do with this animal. But even if it did, how would I know? Beyond that, even if I managed to figure things out—what kind of animal it is, what it eats, how long it lives, how it's evolved—what would I do with that information? I guess that wasn't really what I wanted to know. I could smell something coming from the hole, but it didn't smell like an animal. It smelled more like grass. Maybe it was water. Old, underground water mixed with mold, algae, and tree roots.

I stepped timidly onto the metal circle. It was almost exactly the same size as the hole by the river. Maybe it really was the animal in there. No, it had to be. I was about to ask another question when the man broke into a grin and said, "Oh, wait! Now I remember. You came into the convenience store the other day, didn't you? There were kids all over the place, and you found yourself in a bit of a bind. I did what I could to help. Had to do something, right?" I got the feeling he was waiting for me to thank him, so I obliged. He smiled again and said, "No, no. It was my pleasure." I could see all of his teeth. "When I saw you at the store, I had no idea you were Mune's bride. So I take it you're not fond of kids. More interested in animals, right? Are you scared of children? Or is it the other way around? You love them? When people are indifferent to kids, you can really see it. They'll act the same whether they're around kids or not. That's how it is with the guy who works construction. He comes into the convenience store to get his lunch, but it's like he doesn't even see them. He just steps over them or pushes them out of the way to grab what he needs. But you—you just froze. If you act that way, kids are bound to react. They feed off that stuff. They're not trying to be mean or anything. They're just bored. They're good kids. All of them. They love playing by the river. You must have gone past the spot on your way to the store . . . This place. Talk about the middle of nowhere, right? In this day and age, walking that far just to get to the store? Well, at least it's there now. Before the store opened, the kids had to go all the way to the farmers' co-op to get ice cream. We couldn't read manga unless we went to the bookstore, and that's way too far to walk. This store is a godsend! The store and the river—those are our main battlegrounds. Which probably means I'm not a real hikikomori. I like to come outside and play."

The man barely stopped to breathe. When he did, I said, "I fell into a hole like this the other day." He looked almost offended. "How did that happen? Where?" "Near the river. I followed the animal and fell in . . ." "You're not very bright, are you?" He was practically spitting at me. I didn't know what to say. I had no idea why he was suddenly so upset. "What kind of idiot falls into a hole? Wait, was there anything in there?" I shook my head. "Well, that's a good thing. I'd never do anything like that myself. First, it's dangerous. Second, it's about the stupidest thing you could do. And third, you don't belong there—it's totally pointless. Who do you think you are? Alice in Wonderland? You thought you'd follow a white rabbit down a hole and find yourself at the start of some big adventure? Is that what you thought would happen?" He gave an exaggerated shrug. I was shocked. His shrug looked exactly like Tomiko's. I started to think that he really might be her son—that he might be my husband's brother. But why would they have kept this a secret from me? Didn't we have to tick some box when we got married saying my husband was the eldest son? Didn't we have to fill out some form like that when we made the move out here? Maybe we didn't. Whatever the case, if he really was my husband's brother, then he had been carefully hidden from me. It wasn't the sort of thing that just fails to come up. It's not like he was an estranged uncle or a distant cousin. Can you really hide your brother's existence from your spouse? Is it even possible? And more importantly—why would anyone do it? Were they worried about the world finding out that the family had a shut-in? Or was there more to it than that? As I imagined having to confront them about it, my mind started to drift. I tried telling myself it didn't really matter, but it absolutely did. It's not like we were after some huge inheritance or anything, but what if things got complicated down the line? It could happen. We could lose money—or maybe something else. It wouldn't be the end of the world if something like that happened, but it could be a real hassle. Could this man really be my brother-in-law? Why hadn't anyone said a word about him? What was going to happen as he got older? Was he going to keep on living in a shed in the backyard? How could I ever ask my husband about any of this? *So—you have an older brother?* How could I say anything to his mother? *So—you have another son?* I was getting depressed just thinking about it. It made me feel like an idiot. How would they feel? At the very least, they should have said something when we moved in next door. It's not like we could live here without crossing paths. He lives in a shack right next to me—well, not that I'd ever noticed it here before today. Forget the hole. This was the bigger adventure. "I don't know."

"You don't know?" the man snorted. "That's rich. Well I do—probably because I'm the rabbit." "What?" "I mean, the rabbit Alice went after was no ordinary bunny. It was the Queen's butler—her servant. Right? But, before Alice fell down the hole, it really was just a bunny. I'm sure the English countryside is positively hopping with them! You see what I mean? Before the hole, Alice was just an ordinary girl with a bit of a wild streak. But once she's down there, it's a different story altogether. Now the rabbit's a real character, a working stiff with his own personality. Well, maybe he's more middle management than anything else. He dresses like he has a pretty high station in life. I'm talking about the illustrations. In other words, this run-of-the-mill tomboy gets lost in her own fantasies—some big adventure, right? For you, that makes me the rabbit after the fall." I couldn't make sense of anything he was saying. Without waiting to see if I understood, he forged ahead. "Then again, that's not your story, is it? Yours is no grand adventure. That was no rabbit you went after. It was just this guy," the man said, pointing at the hole. The hand that had been in the wall—the one that he'd been using to play with the child next door—was now as pale as the other. "It's just some stupid animal. Would it make you feel better if we gave him a name? I never thought he needed one, honestly. But now that there are two of us, I guess it'd be convenient if we could call him something, seeing as you want to talk and all. Using the Internet, looking things up. Why bother? We can name him ourselves. Then again, if you ask me, there's a whole lot of things to talk about before that. After all, we're a couple of grown-ups, aren't we? You're not the shrimp next door. Darn! Apologies there! You're a man! A man among men! Anyway, where were we? Right, right. Names. What'll it be?"

"Me?" "Yeah, you. You're the one who fell into that hole. What would you have done if you got stuck in there? Lived together happily ever after?" The whites of his eyes were terribly white. "I don't know what to . . ." "It's just a name! What's yours?" I hesitated for a second. "It's Asahi." "Asahi, eh? Sounds like a cigarette brand from years and years ago. Great! So it's settled. We'll call him Asahi." "What?" "Just kidding. It's a joke.

Anyway, you come up with the name. That'll be your homework. If you can't come up with something good, I'll throw you in the hole, put the lid on, then cover it with a concrete block! Sorry, another joke. Did I scare you? Hey, I'm scared, too. It's been ages since I've talked with somebody who wasn't a kid." "You mean not even Muneaki-san or your mother—not ever?" "That's exactly what I mean. Didn't I just say that? We don't talk, but I can hear her all the time. The kitchen vent lets out right here. She's always calling you Asa, so I had no idea what your actual name was. For all I knew, it could have been Asako or Asami. I never heard anyone answer, either, so I figured maybe you couldn't talk, but that's not the case, is it? By the way, Mom's really put on some weight recently, hasn't she? I can see her clothes when she has the laundry out, and it looks like she's aiming to make it as a yokozuna, doesn't it?"

But wait—what was he eating every day? Where did he get his clothes and shoes? What was he doing for money? I wanted to ask, but couldn't. Then the man clapped his hands together a couple of times. "Alright, let's go. Down to the river. To the hole. I'll be your guide, as a sign of our new friendship. It's really a nice place, this river of ours. Besides, I want to see where you fell in. If it's dangerous, we should probably fill it in. What if one of the kids fell in? They'd never make it back out. Oh wait! Let me wash my face first." The man walked over to the sink outside the shack, wet his hands, then rubbed his face a few times. When he was done, he wiped his face with what looked to be a cloth hanging next to the sink. "'Wash your face three times a day,' right? Don't want to get sticky. This is well water. It's pumped up here. Nice and cold. Tastes good, too. It failed the safety inspection, but I'm the only one drinking it, so who cares? I wasn't planning on living very long anyway. You'd better steer clear of it. Unless you wanna sip? Hahaha. Why would you, right? You can get anything you want from the store. And you've got drinkable water on tap. Okay, all set—shall we? Which way to the hole?" "By the river, on the way to the store." As soon as I said it, he sprang in that direction, not wasting any time. I did my best to keep up. I looked over at the Seras' house. The curtains were drawn. "I bet it wasn't easy for you to climb out of that hole. Was it deep? The deeper the hole, the cooler it is. Warmer in the winter, too. You should see him when he's digging. It's a real show, dirt flying all over the place. You lucked out. Some holes are so deep that they'd be the end of you." "So how does the animal get out?" "Well, it looks a bit funny, but he spirals up, butt first, shimmying up with his feet on one side and back against the other … Wait, is that what you did?" I shook my head.

We followed the walkway to the garden out front, where Grandpa was still watering. He looked at us and opened his mouth. I was sure he was looking at the man, not me. He didn't say anything. His eyes were covered in shadow, but he wasn't making the usual smile. The hose went slack in his hand, water pouring at his boots. The man lifted a hand at Grandpa, who appeared to shake the tip of the hose in response. I guess this means they have to be related. He has to be my husband's brother. Was I supposed to ask Grandpa not to say anything about us being together? What if he said something to Tomiko? Unfazed by my hesitation, my brother-in-law started speaking. "Listen to those cicadas. They're a real earful this year, aren't they?" The second he said it, as if on cue, brown cicadas started roaring all around us. "Inside my shed, I can hear it all. All the sound. I almost feel like I'm becoming one of them." My brother-in-law strode toward the gate. I watched Grandpa standing there, hose pointed downward. He almost looked like a shadow. "How about it, bride? They're pretty loud, aren't they?" "They are. I thought maybe they were like this every year around here …" My brother-in-law snorted. "Hah. Cause we're out in the middle of nowhere? Haha. This is a special summer for them, believe me." I regretted not bringing a hat, maybe even a parasol. I looked up and down the street, at all the houses and windows. I didn't see anyone around. It was almost as if there were some rule against walking outside when the sun was up. Maybe there really was—how would I know? Maybe no one actually lives here. Just me, my brother-in-law, Grandpa, and the cicadas. "He doesn't get along with most folks. Far as I know, he doesn't get along with anybody. I don't even know how he wound up living here. He's a real lone wolf. Not that he's a real wolf." At moments, the cicadas overpowered him and I couldn't hear what he was saying, but I felt like I got the gist.

"Why doesn't animal control do something?" "Animal control?" My brother-in-law looked at me, his eyes wide. "What would they do?" "Well, get rid of it ..." "Why would they do that? He's not doing anyone any real harm." I asked myself why digging holes in the ground that people can't climb out of doesn't qualify as "real harm," but before I could say anything my brother-in-law spat on the ground and said, "Animal control ought to be more worried about the stray cats. There's a whole bunch of them hanging around the house, treating the garden like it's their own personal litter box. A couple of years ago, one of these cats had the nerve to give birth in our garage, then ran off and left the kittens behind. Can you believe it? Then the crows showed up, looking for an easy lunch. I had to stand out there and shoo them away. For a whole day. The mama cat never even came back. But what kind of parent does that? How irresponsible can you be? Now I chase the cats off whenever I see them. I'm sure I'd just look crazy to anyone who saw me, but those things bring nothing but grief."

"You mean everyone just ignores it?" "Ignores what?" "Well, um, the animal ..." "I guess this is why he needs a name. Except, yeah, everyone's always ignoring him anyway. Who knows, maybe they never even noticed him. People always fail to notice things. Animals, cicadas, puddles of melted ice cream on the ground, the neighborhood shut-in. But what would you expect? It seems like most folks don't see what they don't want to see. The same goes for you. There must be plenty you don't see." As we got closer to the river, my brother-in-law was practically jumping sideways. He didn't move like someone who was in his right mind. Maybe my husband and his mother had a reason to hide him from me. "It's tragic. He's been out here this whole time, just digging, with no one to keep him company. I've seen him out here for years, but he doesn't seem to gain or lose any weight. I have no idea how old he is, or how long he's going to live, but he never looks any different. All he does is dig holes, crawl inside, then climb back out. Maybe he's a bit like me. Well, I mean, I've aged a little bit, but ever since I moved out back twenty years ago, not a damn thing's changed. Maybe the girls on the magazine covers at the convenience store, the flavors of Cup Noodles, the lunch options. Now they've even got authentic Szechuan mapo tofu and goya chanpuru yakisoba. Except, at some point, they started charging for salad dressing. You have to pay extra for that." I didn't know how to respond. My brother-in-law wasn't even sweating. He actually looked like he didn't feel the heat at all. His cheeks were pale as ever. He didn't have the slightest tan. Did he have an AC unit inside the shed? He had to. Otherwise he'd die from heatstroke. Maybe he was just used to this kind of weather? He was walking even more strangely now, leaping forward as far as he could, then stamping down hard where he landed. I did my best to stay right behind him, but I had no idea how to keep the right distance.

As we got closer, I could see the riverbank, just like before. The same smell filled my nose. I could see a grassless stretch of sand covered in rocks that I hadn't noticed before. Maybe it was because of the rain we'd had the day before, but the river looked fuller. Even though it was surrounded by houses, the water was anything but muddy—it was clear and green as if we were close to its source. My brother-in-law pointed at something. In the tall grass, I saw a little girl wearing a yellow hat. She leapt out, jumped into the river and splashed her way downstream. A bird that had been walking on the water took flight. I stopped where I was and watched the girl's exaggerated paddling. She dunked her head into the water. Parts of the river had to be deeper than they seemed. Her yellow hat came loose, floating on the surface of the water. When the girl emerged, she rubbed her eyes with both hands. It looked like she was smiling.

As we started walking again, more children appeared on the riverbank, one after another. Some were smaller than others. They were on the bank, in the river, carrying nets for catching fish or insects. They were throwing rocks, chasing small fish, yipping with delight. A few were wearing swim caps and trunks. At the edge of the water, little shoes were lined up in pairs. There were children with fishing rods in their hands and baskets at their hips. Their rods strained as they pulled in fish that looked blue in the light. In their creels, I saw heads and tails.

Deep in the grass, I saw something dark, moving quietly. It was the heads of children. Weren't they worried about ticks? Did they ever get cut by the grass? In a fortress of leaves, it looked as though children were playing a game, but I had no idea what the rules were. Every now and then, a child would shout something and hop out into the open. When this happened, the others would break into laughter. Then the one who jumped out would start counting while the others hid in the bushes. Another group was playing house. Pairs of girls were picking wildflowers and sticking them in each other's hair.

I could see violence, hear consolations. Reconciliation. Pain and anger dissolving in a deafening chorus of rock, paper, scissors. What was going on? Where had all these children come from? Why were they playing here like this? "It's summer break." "Summer break?" My mouth fell open. He was right. It was summer vacation. In my day-to-day life, I never really thought about what the date was—not anymore. I knew the day of the week. I had to know when to put out the trash and when the big sales were. But aside from that, I'd lost track of time. "It's almost Obon. If they're not playing, what else can they do?" Obon. We'd be visiting my parents soon. I'd set it up to coincide with my husband's time off—Obon was just around the corner. I barely ever looked at my schedule now. My planner was stashed in my bag, together with that stupid 30,000-yen bonus from my old job. I know I brought my bag when we moved, but couldn't even remember where I'd left it. Had I even looked at a calendar in the last two months? Where did the days go? Boys and girls were singing "The Cuckoo." I couldn't hear them very well, but I was pretty sure they weren't singing the actual lyrics. Some older children were having younger ones build a dam out of rocks. Taking everything in, I kept on walking. The sky was blue and I could see large clouds hovering in the distance. The grass was green and the water was clear. A large bird swooped into the river and the children cheered and shrieked. In a voice full of pride, my brother-in-law asked, "What do you think? It's a nice river, a wonderful river. A treasure trove of wildlife. A play place for children . . . Believe it or not, it used to be even more beautiful, back when I was a kid. In those days, the river was full of sweetfish, but now it's mucked up with wastewater from all the houses and high-rises. Then again, not all is lost. The birds still migrate here. We get a lot of fish, too. No sweetfish, but lots of little guys no larger than your thumb. We have plenty of insects, too. Mole crickets, dragonflies, grasshoppers with wings and legs missing. The kids are always catching them, then cutting them loose. If there's anything you want to know about the river, ask away. I'm your man. Everyone else graduates. They grow up and move on. They stop playing here, stop coming to read comics at the store. I'm the only one who's in it for the long haul."

"Sensei!" a shrill voice cried. A few boys ran up the bank toward us. One of them was carrying a one-liter plastic bottle. "Sensei, look! Sensei!" "Are you their teacher?" My brother-in-law shrugged at my question and said, "I told you. I'm unemployed." Then he got closer and spoke quickly and softly so no one else could hear. "What else could kids call a grown-up who spends all day playing with them? I'm too old for them to call me by my name, and it's not like I want them calling me 'sir' or anything like that. They're just sticking to what they know—and I'm not sinister enough to make them do otherwise." Before he could even finish speaking, the boy with the bottle spoke up. "Sensei!" He held up the bottle so my brother-in-law could see. It was dry inside, with black centipedes crawling around, climbing upward, then tumbling back to the bottom. The boys seemed to enjoy it. My brother-in-law grabbed the bottle, held it up to the light, tilted it sideways to get a better look, then handed it to me. It was heavier than I expected. The centipedes climbed over each other as they moved up the sides of the bottle. I could feel them wriggling, their tiny movements tickling my palm. One of the boys said, "Nana's gonna soak 'em in oil!" Then another one said, "And it's gonna smell real bad when she does." I looked closer. The centipedes had white parts on their backs. "Gross," I said—to the boys' dismay. The one closest to me snatched the bottle back and quickly stuffed it under his shirt, revealing a suntanned stomach. I could hear little legs in motion, squeaking against the plastic. "They're great centipedes! Real specimens!" my brother-in-law said, scratching at the corner of his mouth. "Hey, don't let the centipedes bite!" "Who cares if they do? That's what the centipede oil's for!" "But that stink is out of this world! The smell will kill your nose dead!"

In the distance, I heard fireworks going off. A black dragonfly glided over the surface of the river. A boy swung his net at it, but the dragonfly darted away, then landed gently on the water. While we walked, I asked my brother-in-law a question: "What made you want to leave the house?" He put on a sad face for only a second, then broke into a broad smile. With his teeth showing, he really did look just like Grandpa. "We didn't see eye to eye!" he said as he tried not to laugh. "What can I say? They're not bad people. I know that. Mom, the rest of them, they're all good folks. I'm an upstanding citizen myself—wouldn't hurt a fly. Anyway, no one's to blame. It's just, families are strange things, aren't they? You have this couple: one man, one woman. A male and a female, if you will. They mate, and why? To leave children behind. And what are the children supposed to do? Turn around and do the whole thing over again? Well, what do you do when what you've got isn't worth carrying on? The things people do for family. My old man worked himself to the bone, my mom always took care of Granny—no blood relation of hers. And they never got along. Granny died when she was pretty young, but dying is no simple matter. A lot of things happened before the end. Mom's still looking after Gramps, and he doesn't really get along with anybody. I guess it never ends. She's always putting someone else first. Seeing everything my parents did to keep the family going ... It's a little spooky. Well, it spooked me out. Know what I mean? Maybe you don't, and I guess that's for the best. One rebel per household, right? I couldn't handle it, so I got out ... Fortunately, I had a little brother with a good head on his shoulders. He found a bride of his own. It's a real relief. I mean it, from the bottom of my heart. Then again, if you think about it, what's the source of that relief? I guess on some level I'm happy that my bloodline isn't going to stop. It's a bit complicated, right? And a little embarrassing at this age! Even downright shameful. What a shameful life! Look at me, the family disgrace, hidden from my little brother's bride and all ..." The buildings on the opposite bank were starting to look familiar. This had to be the place. "I think it was right around here . . ." I looked around, but couldn't find the hole. My brother-in-law kicked at the grass with the toe of his shoe, but there was nothing there, not even a click beetle.

Two children popped their heads out of the grass. "Sensei! What are you doing?" "Sensei, is that your wife?" My brother-in-law put a finger to his lips to shush them. "Don't go starting rumors! You want to get sued? She's my brother's bride." "Your brother's bride!" "What's she like?" "She's a real good person." "Sensei, what are you guys doing?" "We're looking for a hole. Have you seen one?" "A hole?" the kids repeated in unison as they looked at each other. "This place is full of holes! They're everywhere." One of them leapt up, then vanished underground. The other child and my brother-in-law broke out laughing. Suddenly there were holes everywhere. The child had slipped inside one and was shaking with laughter. "Holes all around us!" And there really were. Some were narrow and others were wide; some were shallow and others were deep. There were holes partly covered with grass, almost like traps, and narrower ones that looked as if they'd been scooped out with some sort of tool. One hole was brimming with dirty water, trembling. Bugs were hatching on the surface. Children popped up all around me, wriggling out of their holes. My brother-in-law twisted in laughter. "Um, the animal . . ." "Sensei, I think your brother's bride is trying to say something!" "I'm not going in!" My brother-in-law was shrieking. He screamed again and again. "I'm not going in! No holes for me!" I tried to find the hole I'd fallen in, but none of them seemed like the right one. "Full of holes! Full of holes!" I felt like I couldn't stand there any longer, watching my brother-in-law howl with laughter. I made my way up the bank alone, assuming he'd follow me, but he didn't. He didn't say a thing. As I walked up the path, it looked like there were even more children playing by the river. Some were wearing tank tops and underwear. Another group was doing a weird dance, and several other kids were gathered in a circle around a boy defecating on the ground. As soon as I got home, I looked out the window to see what Grandpa was doing. He was in the garden, pointing the hose upward, covering the grass in mist. A rainbow fell over him.

JUST LIKE MY BROTHER-IN-LAW HAD SAID, IT WASN'T long until Obon. My husband and I drove out to see my parents. It was just the two of us in the car. On the way, there were so many times I thought about asking my husband about his brother, but I decided against it. What would I do if he said they weren't brothers? If that were true, then who was he? And what would I do if they were brothers? How could I respond to that? What could I say? I pretended that the jazz he was playing had put me to sleep. We spent two nights with my mom and dad. When we got back, my husband still had one day off, which he used to go out with friends from his school days. He invited me, but I passed—as he knew I would. Tomiko had work off, too, so Grandpa stayed out of the garden. He had to be in the house, in front of the TV, sleeping the day away. In the evening, Tomiko went out to water the plants. The whole routine took her less than ten minutes. Once Obon was over, my husband and Tomiko went back to work.

In the middle of the night, I heard a sound in the dark. It wasn't loud, not at all, but it woke me up. I got out of bed and looked out the window. The ring of light outside Tomiko's house flickered for a moment. Looking toward the gate, I thought I saw someone under the neighbors' running lights, heading out to the street. It looked like Grandpa. I turned to my husband. Asleep. He was almost like a porcelain doll.

I quietly left the room, hurried downstairs, slipped into my shoes, and walked out the door. Nothing was going on at Tomiko's. Maybe no one had noticed Grandpa leaving. I looked around to see if I could find him, but it was too dark. There were only a few streetlights and a couple of houses with lights on. He wasn't in the light. I looked all around, into the thick darkness. I thought I could feel something move—a shift in the air—so I ran in that direction. It had only taken me a couple of seconds to run downstairs, put my shoes on, and come outside. I told myself that I should be able to catch up with him, as long as I didn't run in the wrong direction. I was running as fast as I could, almost tripping over my own feet, when I saw someone's back a few steps ahead of me. "What are you doing out here?" It was my brother-in-law. "I thought I saw . . ." "Gramps? He's right there, walking." I saw my brother-in-law's bright white shirt sleeve rise up and point ahead. It really was Grandpa, striding forward. He was moving with purpose, as if he knew exactly where he was headed. I turned to my brother-in-law. "Where's he going?" "How would I know?" He sounded annoyed. "I was in the garden. That's the only reason I saw him. But I guess I wasn't the only one who did." "Me? I was in bed, but I heard something, so . . ." "Really? You must have a good ear. Do you have perfect pitch?" I shook my head. Apparently pleased, he said, "Me neither." I couldn't see the moon or a single star in the darkness overhead. All the houses on the street were silent. No cicadas. My brother-in-law stopped talking. I said nothing. Grandpa was walking even quicker now. I was afraid to walk that quickly, but tried to keep up.

Grandpa headed down the path toward the river and we followed closely behind. There was almost no light. It was cold. There were no cicadas, but I could hear insects all around us. It was as if the sound was coming from underground. It couldn't have been crickets. Whatever was making the sound had to be much smaller. It rose up from the river, from the weeds on the bank, filling the air. Cold air crept up the sleeves of my old T-shirt, giving me goose bumps. My brother-in-law looked bored as he walked. I wanted to tell Grandpa it was time to head back, but he moved with such certainty that it made me hesitate. If there was somewhere he wanted to go, I felt like I had to let him. In the dim glow of the streetlights and the lights from the cars across the river, I strained my eyes to get a better look. From what I could see, it didn't seem like Grandpa was in his pajamas. Was that a polo shirt? My brother-in-law was in his usual outfit—leather shoes and all. His white shirt practically glowed in the dark. His shoes scraped against the concrete pavement, but Grandpa didn't turn around. My brother-in-law sneezed loudly—but Grandpa still didn't seem to notice.

After some time, Grandpa took a sudden turn off the path, heading down toward the overgrown bank. For a moment, the sound of the insects stopped, then started buzzing even louder. Grandpa had disappeared. Every once in a while, headlights across the river cast light on the water. "He got in," my brother-in-law said as he came to a stop. "He got in?" I asked. He didn't respond. All I could do was head down the bank after Grandpa. Something snapped under my shoe. Small bugs flew in my face. I held my breath and walked slowly down the uncertain slope. With every step, I felt hard and soft things underfoot. Grasshoppers shrilled, then flew into the air. A large bird standing by the edge of the river appeared to be emitting its own light. In the darkness, I saw a large hole—only Grandpa's head was showing. He was looking in the direction of the river. I dropped into the empty hole next to his. I felt like I had no choice. I stepped on something soft. I looked down and saw a pair of eyes looking up at me, blinking. It was the animal. I felt a cool, moist air coming up from the bottom of the hole. It didn't smell, but I could feel its stiff fur through the legs of my pajamas. I could tell that it was breathing. The sky looked both distant and near. Gravity seemed heavier, but my body felt lighter. A bird that looked particularly large from my vantage point stretched its neck, shook its head, then went still again. The buzz of insects sank into my gut.

"You know ..." I could hear my brother-in-law above us. "I never thought Muneaki would come home. I thought he hated it." "Hated what?" "This. This place, this family." He sneezed again. It looked like Grandpa was staring at the sky. From where I was, I could only see the back of his head. I couldn't tell if he could hear my brother-in-law or not. "I mean, what's to like? Think about it. I put him through a whole lot. A whole lot. It was hard on all of them. Mom, Dad, Gramps. Maybe it's a good thing Granny passed before I got this way ... It's a sad state of affairs. I know I'm talking about myself, but I guess part of me has always felt like it was someone else, even now." The headlights on the other side of the river disappeared. The river went black. Together with the insects, I could hear something moving slowly. Maybe it was the water. Maybe the wind was picking up. As soon as the thought crossed my mind, a cold breeze blew in from the water—colder than it ever was in daytime. "If it were me, I probably would have put more distance between myself and this place. I guess he couldn't do it, and honestly it's a real weight off me. I heard he was coming back—and then he really did. It's a bit strange to say this, and it's not like I've been looking on from beyond the grave or anything, but ever since he moved back, I've watched him go to work every morning and then come home. In my own way. Just like mom, really ... I guess it's weird, but we're only human. That's life, right? I wouldn't wish it on you, but it was your choice after all, wasn't it?" "What was?" "This. This current that never stops. Everything I wanted to escape from." I could see ripples on the water, but I couldn't tell where the light was coming from. Little waves formed one after another, each with its own shape. I could hear Grandpa breathing heavily. Maybe he was cold. I know I was. I had to get him home, right away. "Bride—please don't think badly of them for hiding me away. It's me. I'm the bad one."

As cars appeared on the road again, I could see the outline of the grass across the bank. The large bird flew up, then plunged into the river. Lit up by the flash of the headlights, it looked bright red. The water rippled, then became quiet again. The bird didn't return to the shore. I could hear the animal breathing by my feet as if it were asleep. I tried lifting myself out, but my hands sank into the wet soil. I tried kicking off the wall. When I did, the bottom of my foot bumped the animal's snout. It jerked up as I rolled out of the hole. I could hear the animal inside, breathing, moving. I looked down, but it had already dissolved into darkness. I reached out to Grandpa and said, "Let's go home." He turned his eyes from the sky to me. It must have been the first time our eyes had really met. He groaned as he gave me his hand—it was damper and hotter than I thought it would be. His palm felt hard as a rock, his arm heavy. The soil squelched between my hand and his. I put all my weight into pulling him out. His hand in mine, I led Grandpa up the slope. He followed obediently. "This moon's too good to pass up," my brother-in-law said, "I'm staying here for now." I looked up, but didn't see the moon anywhere. Nothing but clouds. "If that's what you want. Just be safe. We're heading home." While we walked, I thought I could hear children rustling in the grass. I turned around a few times, but never saw anyone. Maybe it was just the insects.

When I got Grandpa home, I stepped into the entryway and called for Tomiko. The door inside was unlocked. Tomiko came down and so did her husband. I hadn't seen him in so long. Even during Obon, he was out playing golf. He didn't look the way

I'd remembered him. In his loose, blue pajamas, he looked thinner than before. He and Tomiko were staring at me in wonder. A yellow light fell on them, casting deep shadows on Tomiko's face. She looked worn out.

"What's going on?" "Grandpa went outside, just now. I saw him leave, so I went after him and brought him back." "Grandpa," Tomiko said in a high-pitched voice, placing one hand on his shoulder. "You're as cold as ice," she said to him, glaring at me. "It's got to be freezing out there. Grandpa, where were you trying to go?" He didn't answer. He looked tired, almost asleep. I watched while Tomiko tried to get Grandpa to look her in the eye, but he wouldn't. Still, he had to be looking at something. At different moments, his pupils grew larger and smaller. Tomiko gave up and looked at me. This time she put on a faint smile, so I did the same. "Thank you, Asa," she said. Then she muttered in a lower voice, "I don't know how I didn't notice . . ." "I don't know how I did." I said good night and closed the door behind me. On the other side, I could hear Tomiko saying something, but it was too quiet to make out. Her husband's voice was louder, but still indistinct. When I got home, my husband was still sound asleep. I crawled into bed. I could feel the mattress under my back rise and fall with his breaths. After that, Grandpa got a fever, which soon gave way to pneumonia. Tomiko took him to the hospital and he died not long after.

FROM AROUND NOON, MY IN-LAWS' FRONT DOOR WAS left open. Old men and women I'd never seen before filtered slowly into the house. They took off their shoes and offered their condolences. Most of them stepped up from the entryway with one hand on the shoe closet and the other on their knee. It had never occurred to me how hard it would be to get into their house if you had bad knees. There was no handrail, no platform. Grandpa did it every day, on his own. He must have had very strong legs. The old women all looked so different. Their hair was white, dyed jet black, or even bright purple or yellow. They were wearing their regular clothes. No one was carrying bags, but they all had prayer beads. I didn't know where I should be, so I hovered around, standing in the entryway, then I moved to the kitchen before coming back out again. I bowed to our elderly visitors, who probably knew as little about me as I knew about them. They still mumbled in my direction, then nodded meaningfully. When they did, I bowed again, saying things like "I know, it was so sudden," at which they'd inevitably tear up and touch my shoulder compassionately. When I found a moment to slip away, I went looking my husband, who was still in his suit from work. I whispered, "Who are these people? Relatives? Neighbors?" "I really don't know," he said. In the altar room, he asked his mother the same question. Once she'd explained things to him, he came back and told me she said they were probably neighbors. "Probably?" "She said there are a few people she's not sure about . . ." My husband whispered, unabashedly studying the faces of the strangers around us. The altar room was full of the elderly. Is this normal? Is it normal for an entire neighborhood to show up and view the body on the day somebody dies? The car from the funeral home had just brought him back from the hospital. It wasn't even a formal wake. It wasn't something I'd ever heard of before, but apparently they read sutras at the bedside of the dead. It occurred to me that no one in my immediate family had ever died. Some of the visitors broke down crying. Others went up to see the body together. One of the mourners had a towel wrapped around his neck like a farmer in the field. When someone else pointed it out, the old man quickly grabbed the cloth and stuffed it into the elastic waist of his pants together with the hem of his jacket and started mumbling in prayer.

Over only a few days, Tomiko's exhaustion had started to show. I'd spent more time at the hospital with Grandpa than she had. Of course I did. She had to go to work. Tomiko would put in a full day at work, or at least half, then rush straight to the hospital, which was enough to take it out of anyone. A few times, Tomiko stared at someone's face, realized what she was doing, then bowed deeply. In response, the old people would nod repeatedly. There were small people and angular people. Under a pristine white sheet provided by the funeral home, Grandpa's eyelids were turning whiter by the second. My father-in-law told us he was hurrying back, but he hadn't arrived yet. The only people there when Grandpa died were Tomiko, Tomiko's sister, and me. No one from his own bloodline.

"Matsuura-san!" one of the old women cried shrilly. I thought maybe she was speaking to me, but she was looking at Tomiko. I had started to get up, but sat down again. Tomiko was looking at Grandpa, completely unaware of the woman calling her name.

The room fell quiet again. "Matsuura-san ... Matsuura-san!" The voice was louder now, but Tomiko still didn't seem to hear it—she was dabbing at the corner of her eye with a handkerchief. I had to do something, so I stood up and asked, "Can I help?" "On the altar, the flowers ..." said a gray-haired woman in a dark red cardigan. "It should be one flower. One flower in each." A puff of air came out of her with every word. The gray faces around her nodded in solemn agreement as they fingered their prayer beads. I looked to Tomiko for help, but she didn't seem to notice. Then another old woman said to me, as politely as she could, "In times like this, you're supposed to have a single flower in each vase. That's how we do it around here." "Maybe they do it differently elsewhere." "So what if they do?" "It should be one flower. One flower only." Pale fingers moved rhythmically over two strings of glass beads. On either side of the altar was a vase painted dull gold with white chrysanthemums inside that Tomiko had asked me to buy. Tomiko had taken out the fake flowers, washed out the vases, and then placed four chrysanthemums of varying heights in each. I stepped toward the altar and grabbed the vases. They were heavy with water. "One in each?" I asked, unsure where to direct my question. Countless grandmothers nodded in unison. As I left the room, I could feel eyes on my back. I heard Tomiko calling me, but kept going. Behind me, I could hear someone whisper. "Ah, he lived a long life, a very long life." A higher voice continued. "His wife must have been lonely, waiting for him on her own all this time." "He lived a good, long life." "He was, what, eighty-nine? Ninety?"

I took the vases into the kitchen and put the flowers with the shorter stems in a cup that had been upside down in the dish drainer. As I filled the cup, the water turned white. It was still going to be a while before the priest would arrive. With one vase in each hand, I went back to the altar, being careful not to spill the water. When I got to the room, it looked like there were even more old people than before. They were surrounding Grandpa, practically on top of one another. Were there really this many old people living in the area? I only saw two children, and both of them looked like they were on the verge of falling asleep. Sera was there, too. I nodded at her and she nodded back. At her side, copying the way she sat on her legs, was a small boy. The boy was also holding hands with the old woman on his other side. The woman stared straight ahead. The Sera woman was wearing the same white blouse as before—in a crowd of muted colors, she stood out. The boy's face was bright red. As I made my way to the altar, an old woman with a small, hoarse voice said, "It's one flower until the funeral. After that, just make sure it doesn't die ..." Her words sounded like a prayer. As I set the vases down, voices filled the room. "Turn it around ..." "No, turn it, flip it so—that's right." I tried to do as I was told. The chrysanthemums leaned stiffly to the side. It occurred to me I should have kept the shorter stems and left the longer ones in the kitchen. "What happened to the flowers?" Tomiko asked me. "It's a wake," I whispered, "so there's supposed to be one flower in each vase. Well, that's what they said." Tomiko didn't seem convinced, but didn't say anything else. She looked at the flowers, then at Grandpa. On the hospital bed, they'd closed his mouth, but his front teeth were poking out now.

"The priest's here," one of the old men said. "It's the young priest." "The young one, huh?" "Well, you know, the master's knees and all ..." "We had him come the other day and he showed up in a wheelchair. But this was Grandma, so it had to be the old priest, even if he had to crawl across the tatami." "But the young priest has a good voice ..." "Well, when it comes to voices, the younger the better." "Almost ninety ..." "A good, long life ..." "Where's his son? Still not home?" The man who came in was dressed in black and looked to be around fifty. I'd never seen him before. He was wearing strangely shaped glasses. My husband opened the glass door to the altar room so he could come in. The priest brushed away his robes, removed his sandals, and stepped inside. Over the toes of his tabi, I saw red spider mites—too many to count. Our guests bowed at the priest, and I did the same. When I looked up, Grandma's photograph leapt into my eyes. It wouldn't be long before Grandpa joined her there. She died so long before him that there was no way they would look like a couple. Not that he'd look like her father, either—but they'd clearly look like family. As soon as the priest sat in front of the altar, positioned between the disobedient chrysanthemums, he launched into an unfamiliar sutra. I laid a string of prayer beads across my palm, and the old women around me began chanting in low voices. I could feel something like relief wrapping around my shoulders. When my father-in-law came quietly into the room, the old men and women lowered their heads while reciting the sutras.

Once the priest had finished, the man from the funeral home reappeared. He had all kinds of documents and pamphlets for us. All sorts of things had to be decided for the wake—flowers, refreshments, a whole range of qualities and quantities to be considered. By the time everything had calmed down, it was late at night. After the priest left, our aged guests went home one or two at a time, until the only ones remaining were the closest relatives. There were tissues scattered across the tatami. When I went to pick them up they were wet. I gathered them and tossed them in the trash, along with a few discarded candy wrappers. My parents were supposed to come before the wake the following evening. Tomiko sighed. "It was hard when Grandma passed, too, but Grandpa took care of everything . . ." She said the same thing a few times over, but by the end was whispering so softly I could barely hear what she was saying. Her sister ran over to hug her. "We should be grateful. He wasn't sick for long. It's better this way, not spending a long time sick in bed. Pneumonia—most people who make it to old age die of pneumonia. What matters is whether or not you suffer before the end." "I know. It just happened so fast . . ." Tomiko kept talking, but I couldn't hear what she was saying. Her sister was upbeat. "People that age hope to go quickly. Remember what it was like with Grandma? Living like that, not even conscious, for as long as she did . . . At least he had his health, right up to the end. He could get around on his own—he stayed sharp, too, mentally."

Then Tomiko looked right at me. I looked back at her. Grandpa watering the plants flashed in my mind. The sun was behind him, so I couldn't see his face—only his teeth. Only a few hours after dying, his dark skin had clouded white. It was almost glowing. We exchanged glances for a moment, then Tomiko spoke. "You're right," she said, "you're right." I got up to make tea for our guests. I could smell the six chrysanthemums in the wide-mouthed cup sitting by the sink. Each stalk was still hard with a life all its own. For the first time, I started to wonder if my brother-in-law would come to pay his respects. Of course he knew what was happening. People had been coming in and out of the house all day, and the smell of incense had practically filled the neighborhood. Even if he didn't get along with the rest of the family, he could hardly hang around behind the house, acting like this had nothing to do with him. Once I'd made the tea and served it to everyone, I quietly headed out back. The shed was dark. Maybe he was sleeping. I put my hand on the sliding door and rattled it. Locked. I'd barely touched the door, but the whole shed shook. It smelled like mildew. Looking over at the old well, the metal grill was missing—and in its place was a large concrete block partly covered with moss. I tried the door again, then knocked. No response. There was bright red rust on my fingers. The handle was covered in dust. The air around me was full of children's voices and shrill cries and the smell of old men and women. They washed over me, then slipped away. Once I was back inside, Tomiko was sitting exactly the way she had been. Relatives were getting ready to go home for the night. My father-in-law stood up and bowed.

"It doesn't matter what you're going through, the stomach wants what it wants. We should eat something ..." When Tomiko finally got up, she looked in the fridge. She pulled out what had been a green onion, the tip brown and withering from days of neglect. She held it up and gave me a wry smile. I smiled back. "I guess it's too late for this one." I left and went into the altar room to collect the empty teacups. My husband was next to Grandpa, in a daze, sitting cross-legged with his eyes on his phone. His fingers were moving slower than usual. My father-in-law was inside, resting. "What kind of grandfather was he?" I asked as I loaded the cups onto a tray. My husband looked at me with surprise. "Huh?" "Your grandpa. What kind of grandfather was he?" "Grandpa?" My husband put his phone on the tatami, rubbed his hands together for a second or two, then grabbed his phone and started moving his fingers. "I used to think he was scary. But I remember, when I got into college, he was so happy that he gave me 300,000 yen. 'Don't tell your mom,' he said. In cash, fresh bills—not that I had them for long ..." "What did you get?" "I don't remember. Probably nothing special." "What did he like to do?" "Grandpa? For fun? Well, we went fishing a few times, but I don't think he liked it all that much. It was a little awkward, really. We never caught anything." I looked down at Grandpa, then up at his wife. "What makes you ask?" "Nothing." When I went back to the kitchen, Tomiko had chopped up some onion. Pouring soy sauce into a pot, she said, "He was a good dad."

We had somen in hot soup—though I wasn't sure if this would be considered dinner or a late-night snack. While we ate, Tomiko blew her nose again and again. "Dad's not eating?" "He said he'll have some later." As usual, my husband wouldn't put his phone down, even when holding his chopsticks. Once he was done with his soup, he stood up, cracked his neck, then went back into the altar room. "What about a bath?" "Later." I finished eating, put my husband's bowl in my own, and carried them to the sink. "Just leave them like that. I'll do it." "It's fine, I can do it." "No, really. I'll do it right now," Tomiko said, but she wasn't getting up. I wet the sponge under the faucet and looked at the chrysanthemums leaning against each other in the cup. I couldn't smell them over the green onions. I washed everything in the sink. "Sorry," I heard Tomiko say. I didn't say anything back. The bowls we'd just used, the bowls with strings of natto inside that looked as though they'd been there for a couple of days, the light-colored china cups we'd used for tea—all of them were handpicked by Tomiko, or maybe even by Grandma. I turned the water up a little and washed away the bits of onion and tea leaves in the sink. As water sprayed out of the faucet, the chrysanthemums jostled beside me. Their smell hit me again. For some reason, my husband struck the bell. Through the vent, I could hear my brother-in-law laughing. I thought I could hear another voice, too. When I looked back at Tomiko, she was resting her cheek in her palm, eyes closed and drifting off to sleep. I watched her back rise and fall. She'd probably be asleep for a while. After washing the dishes, I went out back again. No one was there. The shed was dark. Same as before. I tried the door. After a moment's resistance, it opened. The smell hit me right away. Dust and mildew. It was dark inside, but I could see all kinds of shapes, stacked up, against the walls, on the floor. It looked like no one had been there in a very long time. I could see large glass jars lined up on the floor—and something coiled up among them. It looked like there were centipedes inside the jars. Hanging from the ceiling was a bare light bulb. I tugged on the cord, but no light came on. The bulb dangled slowly overhead. When I tried a second time, something dusty rained down on me, so I ran outside. I'd only been inside for a few seconds, but when I looked at my hands and shoes they were covered in white.

SUMMER WAS COMING TO AN END—IT WAS ALREADY FALL according to the calendar—but every day felt hotter than the last. Was it ever going to cool down? Even the cicadas were as loud as they'd been at the height of summer. Was this really unusual or was it going to be like this every year? Was the climate changing? Was this year an exception? I'd never heard of so many people dying from the heat before. I saw a dead cicada in the middle of the path. Its legs pointed to the sky, its back against the blistering black asphalt. I tilted the handlebars of my brand-new bike and aimed for the insect. I thought it was going to be dry, but it stuck to the front tire, buzzing with every rotation. Was it just air coming out of its belly or was it still alive? I kept pedaling. I hadn't realized it when I was walking, but the path home from the store sloped upward. With every bump and dip, the 7-Eleven uniform in the basket in front of me hopped into the air. I pedaled harder. "There's nothing to do here. We never get any customers. Still, somebody's got to work the register." "But what about all the children?" "What children? Everyone around here is retired. I'm sure it'd be different if we had an office building or a school around here," said the woman with brownish hair as she stood up. "So, you'll start tomorrow." I got up and bowed. As soon as I left the store, the hot air and the smell of grass surrounded me. Old people in overalls were mowing the grass on the riverbank. There was something else mixed in with the thick smell of grass—something familiar, but I couldn't place it. The plastic bottle of water I had bought after the interview was sweating, dripping all over. The green bank was red in places. Mown grass had been raked into neat piles, where there were more spots of red. They looked like spider lilies. I saw no animals, no holes, no children. When I got home and put on my uniform in front of the mirror, I couldn't help but see Tomiko staring back at me.